SINS OF THE KIN

FRANK LUCIANUS

CONTENTS

"Are we sure it's him?" Luca Giuliani said, scratching his forehead.

Sofia nodded, puffing a cigar into the confinements of her grandson's office on the ground floor of one of her late husband's mansion. Sofia remembered chosing every little piece in it, from the color of the furniture to its position in the room. Her friends had told her to get into interior design when she was back in Italy many years ago, to which she politely waved off as nothing but a hobby. Her ambitions were set way too high to settle for something as trivial as such.

"Do you have to keep fucking smoking every goddamn minute, grandma?" Luca said, nearly choking.

"Watch your mouth, mio nipote!"

Sofia continued to smoke and observe the young man she raised since Jessica's departure from the world. Luca really had let her have it over the years, and her pity for his dead mother and father were the reason why she dealt with his crap. Now in her late seventies, Sofia was still a beauty. Her silky black hair and green eyes concluded her prettiness. She always had a vision of smoothly executing what she put her mind to nearly to the smallest detail.

"That's him, alright," Sofia said, her face nonchalant as always. "But he looks so different."

She glanced at the picture on her late husband's desk; a small, black and white photograph. It was the face of that Saltinotti figlio di puttana, Jacopo.

Luca looked worried whereas Sofia was able to hide her emotion. Her grandson's face was red, sweating converging on his forehead while his hands were shaking. He looked at the photo again remembering what his grandmother told him of the battles between his mother and Jacopo. The news that broke to him and Sofia fifteen minutes ago was now the elephant in the room: *Jacopo Saltinotti was coming to town.*

"Let's send Vito," Luca said.

"To do what?"

Luca sat, needing his heart rate to slow down. "To fucking find more about why he's here. We can't just buy him a plane ticket and invite him to our home. This could very well be a fucking trap, grandma."

Sofia stood up and stopped across the large mahogany desk where her grandson sat. She bent over and gave him a kiss on his cheek.

"That was the smartest thing you said all day," Sofia said as she began walking away. "I'll see you in the morning."

"But grandma…"

"Don't worry my grandson. We'll take care of it."

A BROKEN FAMILY

The Saltinotti Family

Jacopo and his wife Maria hadn't slept in the same bed for almost a decade now, since she found him cheating on her with some Russian prostitute. Things changed for the worse afterward but they decided not to get a divorce. If they did, then it would give plenty of opportunities for the rivaling families to take action and seize on their misfortune, spelling the end of the Saltinottis. Therefore, the couple lived together and began doing whatever they wanted. They were free to mingle and fuck whomever they wanted, the only rule was to be discreet in order to keep the family in order. Leaders in crumbles meant a family in crumbles, and they agreed to the need of upholding the infamous name of the Saltinottis for honor's sake.

"What are you still doing up, darling?" Maria asked as she entered the kitchen for a glass of water.

Her daughter, Vanessa glanced up from her textbook and smiled. "Studying for an exam mamma."

"Want me to make you one of my famous hot chocolates?" Maria said, glancing at her daughter who always craved the Italian version of the beverage.

"If you're offering—"

"How's Vincent?"

Vanessa looked down at her textbook, a look of sadness and a heavy sigh.

Maria had made the biggest mistake of letting her daughter, Vanessa marry a useless douchebag so young, but it was part of a peacemaking deal to bring the weak Romano and long-time powerbroker Saltinotti families together. Otherwise, there would have been a decade-long war with many bodies lost with the rival Baldinottis and the remnants of Guilianis and Lombardis who were always threats. Instead of war, the Saltinotti and Romanos chose the white flags and decided to marry their children; Vanessa Saltinotti and the only son of the Romano Family, Vincent.

Maria quickly changed topics, "How are you doing in law school?"

Vanessa sighed, "Ok mamma. It's better than high school."

Maria smiled. Her oldest daughter was twenty-four and she was about to graduate from law school at Columbia. It turned out that Vanessa's IQ was much higher than most of her peers, which led to her skipping a few grades.

"Enjoy it sweetheart, because after college, life will hit you really hard and responsibilities begin to exist from thin air."

"You make it sound like a terrible slow death."

"Trust me, you're going to want to work for me after it's all well and done."

"Mamma, I have literally no idea about anything of the lingerie business, I still don't know how to buy a bra that fits."

Maria chuckled. "You don't need to know anything about the products, just about business and that you got plenty from me." She placed the cup of hot chocolate, topped up with cinnamon and four marshmallows on the table, and kissed Vanessa on the top of her head. "Now study, we can't have the future of our family at risk because you failed your exam."

Vanessa slapped her mother on the butt. "Mamma, you got too much of that back there."

"Watch it you, I can be deadly."

"Deadly my ass, mamma."

"At least, I know my bra size and know how to buy one."

Maria left the kitchen and Vanessa stuck out her tongue.

"This Donna, Jesus."

Vanessa turned her attention back to her books and sipped on her drink.

2

TONY THE CHARMER

New York, New York

Tony Lombardi, the son of the late Giovanni (Jessica's brother) began smoking his first cigarette from his pack of Marlboro Reds 100, enjoying the vapors escape his lips that blocked his view of his labyrinth garden. The balcony was his favourite place to be in morning and evening, exceptionally perfect at sunrise and sunset. It was the place he sought the most when he found himself in deep thought.

Behind the young man's muscular frame, spanned a villa across 18,000 square feet and located in the north-east suburbs on New York. It was completely detached from all nearby buildings, a five-meter fence ensuring privacy. Above everything, he was most fond of money, power and influence, yet privacy topped them all. Tony Lombardi was comfortable in the dark and operating from the shadows. *A virtual ghost.* He was unknown even almost to the Lombardis who were in disarray after the death of Jessica and his father Giovanni. But for the people that mattered most, the word was still on the street that his name was one to be feared. To get in trouble with Tony was a death sentence, and anyone who was unfortunate to be in such a situation had a better chance of committing suicide. At only twenty-six, Tony was a prodigy of the game, a criminal mastermind and the true napoleon of organized crime. His crew ran and ruled the surrounding neighborhoods of suburbia New York City; from narcotics to money-laundering in the millions. Tony lead it all and was the youngest crime boss in history.

He put his cigarette out in the ashtray, fuming out its last smoke and went down to the garden. Despite his vast wealth, Tony was a simple young man who enjoyed the small things in life, like the cup of black coffee in the morning grounded using the finest roasted beans from the motherland with a glass of orange juice on the side. The warming morning sun is what he relished the most on his olive skin, His on-again-off-again girlfriend, Tatiana was there doing yoga. Her curves brought joy to his crotch but only when he wanted her. Yet, Tony was not a fan of the wild lifestyle where wealthy people showed off and competed against each other. He found happiness in his company, and that was what made him scary.

"It's time for you to go," Tony said, as he sipped on his cup eyeing down Tatiana. She was his choice for a companion for last evening.

She was pretty but blond. Tony didn't know why he chose her, he was only ever attracted to brunettes, which made these nightly hook-ups more of a convenience for him.

Tony reminisced, remembering little snippets from last evening of them in various positions. He was a demon on the loose seeking only his own satisfaction and somehow that worked for the woman he was bedding, as she reached her climax mere seconds prior to his. He showed no mercy, fucking Tatiana hard from behind with her nice Russian ass faced to him and her head between the pillows. He felt a burning sensation along his back, and thought of how hard she scratched him as they fucked. Her legs were completely locked around his drawing him further inside her.

Now, Tatiana hadn't moved an inch and Tony quickly became irritated, taking a step closer and clearing his throat.

"Hey, did you fucking hear me?"

That was when Tatiana moved in with lightning

speed bolting towards Tony, jumping onto him from the front, locking her legs around his waist and mashing her breasts against his chest.

"Why don't we pick up where we left things last night?" She licked the side of Tony's face and gave his cheek a wet kiss, inhaling his masculine scent. The needs of her vagina grew as the pool of juices were already flowing.

Tony smirked and in one movement, he unlocked her legs and arms and could've dropped her on her yoga mat, but decided for the grass instead. Tatiana's face changed from horny to scared and then shocked when she hit the ground.

"I hate repeating myself," Tony said in a low tone, while Tatiana glance up at him.

Tony sensed her fear and leaned down, inching closer to her face. "So if you want to keep doing this, I suggest you listen to every fucking word of mine and behave, capisce?"

Tatiana nodded so fast, she almost head-butted Tony.

"Very well." Tony gave her a kiss on the lips and corrected his form, standing tall at six-foot four. "Get your things and I'll escort you to the door, shall we?"

From then on, it was a smooth ride. Tatiana was acting either frightened or was absolutely smitten, as she hurriedly gathered her belongings – which weren't much – from his master bedroom and slipped on her panties, then her silky dress, back on, hiding her large and pointy nipples.

"I'll call you." Tony said, not bothering to look her in the eye as he slammed the door shut.

* * *

Tony then headed to the kitchen, his mind on the breakfast. His chef, Nadia was renowned, having worked and headed famous restaurants in Italy and Greece, releasing famous cookbooks and even landing his own TV show. Now at the age of fifty-five, she was slowing down and enjoying the more simplicities that life offered, much like Tony. That was how they connected and eventually led to him accepting the more-than-generous salary that came with this job as his private chef.

"Another one of your time wasters?"

Tony winced, but smiled wickedly, who had more in common with her motherly figure than his private cook.

"A man has needs," he said, shrugging his shoulders and peeking over Antonio's. "It's how I stay focused.

"If you had a special someone in your life, she would help you keep your eyes on where they should be, and your Johnson tucked away where it should stay."

Their laughter echoed through the kitchen and somehow made Nadia flustered.

"I am not in the business of –" He stopped to for a few seconds, careful of his word choice. "Of trivial emotions." He saw Nadia rolling her eyes and ignored it,.

"When's breakfast ready?" Tony asked, trying to change the subject.

"30 minutes, signore," Nadia replied. "Now get out of my kitchen and let me do what I do best unless you want a burnt breakfast?"

Tony put his hands up and retreated slowly, his eyes holding Nadia's gaze. "As you wish, mademoiselle."

3

MY LITTLE DAUGHTER

New York City, USA.

"I will make him an offer he can't refuse."

Vanessa sighed, not believing the bullshit she was hearing. She loved the Godfather, but the image it portrayed of a real mafia family was rubbish, and how they conducted business wasn't accurate either. Nevertheless, it was a masterpiece and one of her favorites. She'd tolerate the few cringe moments for the satisfying ending.

Suddenly Vanessa's phone rang, leaping her out of the zoom she was in. She grunted, paused the movie and picked up.

"Yeah?"

"Hey babe."

Vanessa's eyes widened.

"Hi, Vincent." Her mouth dropped.

Vincent's sexy laugh made her cheeks redden. He had this effect on her, making her coo over him whenever he wanted. He played Vanessa by the string and even if she would never admit it, loved every second of it. It was toxic and she was addicted.

"Can I not call my favorite girl."

"Favorite girl, huh!" Vanessa clenched her fists hard enough for her nails to break. Without saying anything else, she hung up and got up from her bed. She was in her panties and bra and changed quickly into something more sporty. Vanessa Saltinotti left out shortly after with something else on her mind.

Ten minutes later, Vanessa was firing a gun at the range, her gorgeous blue eyes were masked perfectly. She kept shooting at the head, chest and groin of the target. Over and over again, until her clip finished. She dropped her gun, reloaded and continued her assault on the poster until it was covered in holes.

Vanessa pulled the lever and the poster came to her. She removed it and hang up a new one, ready for her tenth round.

Vanessa's father, Jacopo taught her how to handle guns at a young age. She wasn't innocent, not in the slightest, and was well aware of everything going on. She knew her family was different than most. The Saltinotti family was the biggest mafia family present in New York City, taking the top spot from the once-rival Guiliani and Lombardi crime families. It was only fifteen years ago when New York's Italian mobsters were at war and Vanessa heard the horror stories.

The Saltinotti family now ruled the east coast of the United States while dipping their hands in southern Canada. The Mexicans, JaChencans, Dominicans, Irish, Blacks, and others were in their areas and didn't dare coming close to Saltinottis and their new ally, the Colombos. Any attempt would be met with a heavy price to pay.

Vanessa was well aware of the whispers around her house involving new threats. If her parents mentioned something, it meant it was serious. Yet, she was still in the dark and like it that way.

Vanessa Saltinotti put the gun down. Her rage was almost out of her system, so she headed to the gym back at the mansion. She turned to her favorite punching bag, punching with all her might.

* * *

Maria Saltinotti heard her daughter went to the shooting range from one of the guards. Now, Vanessa's loud grunts and noise of the punching bag were reaching ears upstairs. Maria knew better than to approach Vanessa in this state. Instead, she put her gloves on and went downstairs to the gym, which featured a full boxing-ring, several weight machines, a treadmill and other apparatus for the family and the guards.

"I can see you've gotten good." Maria signaled for Vanessa to join her in the ring. "Don't cry when mamma hit your face."

Vanessa stepped into the ring and eyed down the woman who gave her life.

"Let's see what you've got," Maria said, smirking.

4

LUCA'S LIKE HIS ZIO

Upstate New York

Luca Guiliani thrusted hard as he could into the whore underneath him. She was a new addition to one of his family's brothels downtown, apparently of Russian descent, which explained her porcelain skin. He was sweating heavily, like a pig, and struggled to breathe. He slapped the woman's right nipple hard, waiting for the woman to shout at him. But when she didn't, he bit her other nipple, this time harder. Once again, she wasn't fazed. He glanced into the woman's eyes and realised that he was with a diamond; a different kind of woman.

A few seconds after the thought passed, Luca felt his climax coming and with no warning, began spurting inside her. He then dropped on top of her, breathing heavily.

"Sweet Mary," Luca said now turned to the side, away from the woman.

The sound of a train gliding along the tracks could be heard, and the traffic of the city filled the void of silence inside the room.

"Where you from?" Luca asked.

"Serbia."

"I thought so." Luca grabbed a glass of water from the nightstand and gulped it down. "Well," he began, his fingers touching her privates and entering inside. "You're going to get far here in New York, believe me."

The girl smiled revealing her pearly white teeth. Her face mimicked one of hope. She thought she was going to be promoted to a more stable profession.

Luca knew his words had a double meaning. For him, he always created false hope for the new and young girls to keep them edging and in line. His philosophy was that if they thought that they were going to make it, they would try harder to please their clients which ultimately meant better service, and therefore more money.

"Round two?" The woman asked, looking at Luca's limp cock.

He smiled. "If you can get it up with that sexy mouth of yours, then I don't see why not."

With no time wasted, the woman slid down to the end of the bed, bent over and took Luca's cock into her mouth, sucking softly. Her tongue stroked his most sensitive layers majestically.

Luca put his hand on her head; a tight grasp of her blond streaks and groaned, "That's it, baby. Right there."

5

THE CHINATOWN SETUP - PART 1

Chinatown, New York

Tony Lombardi followed a Chinese man through the corridors of an old warehouse. His top bodyguard was behind him with his gun drawn.

The bodyguard stopped in front of a large door that was the same as all the others they passed, only behind this one was what Tony was here for. An Asian guard looked at Tony, who nodded, and then knocked.

"Hai!" was the cue for Tony to enter. Tony's bodyguard remained out front.

An old Chinese man stood up at the end of the table. "Mr. Lombardi, good to see you again," The old man said balancing himself on his cane and then meeting Tony halfway, shaking his hand.

"It is a pleasure to see you again as well, Mr. Lee."

Tony bowed.

Two bodyguards were accompanying Mr. Lee as well as his two children who served as the old man's right hands. Tony thought it was unnecessary but was in no place to comment on how the Triads ran their organization.

"Wang." Tony put out his hand and was met with a glare from the son.

Tony and Wang's relationship was not on the same page as his with Wang's father. Wang despised Tony for reasons unknown and Tony didn't lose much sleep over it. However, he knew should Mr. Lee pass away, then Wang would take over and that would be a war for another day.

Tony shifted his attention from Wang to Mr. Lee's beautiful daughter Chen, often dubbed as 'the Black Princess of the Far East' by those in the streets. Chen had big black eyes and red sexy lips that aided her persona of innocence. Her hair reached the bottom of her butt and body was the complete opposite of halves. The Asian girl had big tits that were out of ratio of her small skinny top frame.

There were rumors that Chen was not as innocent as her face made her out to be. Word around was that she had her first kill at the age of eleven. From there, she was known for torturing her victims to get what her father wanted.

"Good seeing you again, Chen," Tony smirked.

"The pleasure is mine, Lombardi."

"Very well, shall we begin?" Mr. Lee said as he sat again, his guard helping him.

"Of course." Tony said, his eyes lingering on Chen, who returned the gaze.

Everyone took a seat, Wang was on the right of his father while Chen was about to take a seat on his left, before Tony came around and pulled the chair for her.

"Here, let me."

"What a gentleman," Chen said squeezing Tony's bicep. "Thank you very much. I never knew Italians to be such gentlemen."

"You're welcome and don't be a wise ass," Tony whispered.

Tony sat at the far end of the table, opposite Mr. Lee. He unbuttoned his double-breasted Armani suit jacket.

"I heard you're having a bit of trouble in Manhattan," Tony began.

The trouble Tony was referring to were the random acts of violence that were occurring in the 42rd Street district; the neighborhood that was supposed to be under Mr. Lee's control, as promised to him. The

Yazuka were threatening the Triads, making the Chinese fear them more than the Italians.

"We've tried negotiating with them," Lee began, his fingers intertwined and resting in front of his face. "But they keep coming like fucking ants."

"No reason to swear, I understand."

"Don't talk to my father like that!" Wang shouted.

Tony stared at him, standing up. Mr. Lee instantly diffused the situation by shouting at his son in Chinese, which Tony took as a whole load of swearing.

"I'm sorry for my son, he's young and is unaware of the traditions of the business like me and you." Mr. Lee grinned. "I wish he was more like you, sometimes."

Tony smiled; he was younger than Wang by three years.

"Well, that may be true." Tony said sarcastically, crossing his legs, looking over at Wang. "Mr. Lee, I have something of interest to you."

Tony opened a black folder. "I have to admit that before coming here I have inquired about your little problem." He closed it and looked at the old man. "Your number of customers for heroin are at an all-time low. Now, the addicts are being forced to buy from the petty gangs."

"But that isn't our fault," Chen interjected.

"Business isn't about fault, my dear. Your father knows that very well." He turned his chair slightly to

Chen. "But rather it is about mitigating any rising problems quickly and adapting to keep the numbers high and the influence the same."

"So what are you getting at?" Mr. Lee asked.

Tony smiled. "I can hand you this file right here, right now, and your problems will vanish into thin air."

Mr. Lee smiled. "But, of course, everything comes at a price."

Tony nodded.

"And what is it that you're asking for?" Wang asked.

"Twenty percent."

"That is out of the question, that's too much." Wang raised his voice again but Mr. Lee held his hand up.

"It is a reasonable price, Mr. Lee." Tony continued. "If my projections are correct, the gangs will fairly soon-ish claim territory outside of Manhattan. That means you're looking at Brooklyn, Queens, Mr. Lee. The major boroughs are vital for the running of your business." Tony stopped for a few seconds and leaned onto the table. "For twenty percent, all of those headaches can disappear in a heartbeat. But of course, I will help you bring more product out to the streets."

Tony finished and silence took over the room. The head of the Triads, Mr. Lee was met with an important decision. If he chose wrongfully, it could lead to the doom of the entire organization and his family and their futures. Everything he had built would be in ruins.

Tony had the upper hand, he always had it even days before coming into this meeting, and now Mr. Lee just realized that.

"I agree to your proposal, but—" he held a finger in the air. "If I find your information useless, I demand you to cut off one finger. Let's just say it's an old tradition. If one makes a mistake, he must pay with his pinky finger. That's fair, right?"

"I don't believe in such traditions, Mr. Lee. I believe in results. Do we have a deal?"

"Yes, we do."

Tony slid the file across the table and got up, buttoning his jacket. "It's a pleasure doing business with you again, Mr Lee."

Mr. Lee didn't even hear the parting words of his new partner, as all he could see was red. What he read and saw inside the file made his forehead veins show and face red.

Tony glanced at Chen, who was staring at him, trying to fathom what had just occurred. He nodded her goodbye and left the room, his bodyguard followed a step behind.

As soon as the door was shut, Tony heard Mr. Lee shouting, as he had expected. What was in the file would have made any man lose his coolness. To have your own son attempt to overthrow you, put the entire family at jeopardy was breaking news. It was a lesson for anyone in the business, that betrayal always came from those who are closest to you.

A few seconds later, Tony Lombardi heard a single gunshot and couldn't help the grin on his face. He loved this life, the violence and the suspense that came with it. He was ushered in the black sedan outside the building, its windows tinted, and drove off with plans to enjoy meeting Chen again soon.

6

THE INTRUDER

Upstate New York

"What is it, Harry?" Luca answered the phone while petting his cat.

On the other line was his most trusted insider; Harry Johnson, ex-police sergeant and private investigator gone rogue. *They crossed paths when Luca was doing a favor for a business partner by removing Harry, who had been closing in on bringing down the entire organization. Instead of putting old man Harry on ice, Luca found more use for him. It has been four years of fostering a bond that at sometimes been awkward.*

"There's a dog in your back garden," Harry said.

He told Luca the story of how easy it was to listen in on calls without being bugged, something the FBI has been doing for years. Getting a warrant was on the bottom of their list of priorities. Harry spoke in codes and Luca had no problems deciphering them.

Luca's facial expression changed.

"What breed is it?" Luca walked around his office and stood in front of his 50-inch screen TV displaying the view of several CCTV's he had installed. He could see Sofia sipping on a glass of red wine in the living room, the housecleaner polishing the dining set and a guard outside smoking a cigarette. With a flick of the remote, the smaller displays converged into a single view that spanned the screen. Now, the camera had a clear view of the street in front of the mansion. He zoomed around several objects, including Harry's old car.

"A black hound," Harry said, waiting patiently for Luca to spot the person.

Luca switched from the front camera to several back ones that secured the entire back garden. He caught the movement of a large figure, dressed in a black hoodie, tracksuit bottoms and trainers. His hood was up and Luca couldn't see the man's face. The intruder had a heavy built with an average height.

"Get him and bring him inside," Luca commanded.

"My pleasure, Boss."

Luca dropped his phone on the desk, his eyes glued to the scene enfolding in front of him. He saw Harry emerge and slowly stepped closer to the intruder. His form and method reflected years of experience in the service. As soon as he was within range, Harry pulled out a Taser and electrocuted the intruder, who screamed and then dropped onto the ground. Harry glanced up at the camera, smiled and gave Luca a thumbs up.

"Crazy motherfucker," Tony said leaving his office.

They were in what Luca called *"The Bunker."* It was underneath the darkest part of the basement, had metal walls & soundproof. It's purpose was more of an inter-rogation room.

Harry removed the hood off the man, who was chained to a wall and seated on a metal chair. As soon as the man's face was revealed, Luca knew exactly who he was and who sent him.

"Fucking Jamaicans."

Luca nodded to his men to begin torturing him. Harry and Luca stepped back and began watching the swinging of the men's fists brutally strike the man. After dozens of blows, the man was bleeding badly.

Luca signaled for his men to stop, who stepped away, allowing their boss to inch closer. "Son of Kynami "Hatchet", let's talk."

7

THE RETURN OF MR. HATCHETT

Upstate New York

"I have bad news, Mamma," Luca said.

Sofia entered the office and sat opposite of Luca. Meanwhile, Luca was fidgeting underneath his seat while looking at his grandmother. Sofia was calm, smoking her cigar peacefully and slowly.

"I know," she said exhaling circles of smoke.

"Fucking Anansi, the son of Kynami – How in the fucking world did he manage to find us?" Luca said, his veins pulsating in line with his racing heartbeat.

Sofia scoped the situational and in her head had traveled down the many scenarios of how exactly it could have played out.

"You know what this means?" Luca said glancing at his grandmother.

"It means—" She took another puff before continuing, "That Anansi isn't alone."

"So what do we do?"

Sofia smiled. Then, she uncrossed her legs, stood up and began walking out.

"Where the hell are you going, Mamma?"

Sofia turned around, still in the same faze from before. "I leave this up to you grandson," she said continuing on her way to her bedroom, her cigar still burning between her fingers.

8

NADIA'S LISTENING IN

New York, New York

Tony Lombardi fucked his new plaything of the night viciously. His muscles were burning and straining at their limit, but he ignored it and re-focused on the female that was the cause for his immense pleasure.

They've been fucking for a long time; the red-haired companion now squeezing her legs around Tony's waist, pulling him deeper. The bed synced with their movements and kept hitting the wall, causing bangs that echoed through the room and into the hall outside, along with their groans and moans.

In the last room down the hall, Tony's chef Nadia had attempted several times to sleep but to no avail.

37

The noise of the intense love-making kept her awake and she couldn't help but let her imaginary side of being a chef go wild and firmly envision her employer, glistening in sweat. She blinked several times and gazed at the ceiling, punishing herself for those overcoming thoughts.

She heard another loud bang followed by a series of moans, making the old woman bite her bottom-lip and toss onto her back. She closed her eyes again, her breathing deepening as she now imagined Tony over her, nibbling on her neck. The images that flashed in her mind were lucid and so vivid that she could firmly smell his scent. Nadia couldn't hold back longer as she allowed her hand to grasp her breast while the other travelled down inside her nightgown. She cursed her boss as she began rubbing herself, grunting at the touch of pleasure.

Tony grunted loudly as he pulled out. He was about to ejaculate but held on as he sought the finish of this fuck session, thus getting a hold of Monica's legs and pushing her onto her stomach. Her face was buried in the pillow and her ass was high up.

Tony licked his lips and smacked one of Monica's ass cheeks, seeking pleasure from hearing her howl his name. He entered her, making her scream and holler. Twisting her hair, Tony pulled on it while continuing fucking the red-haired wickedly, like a man possessed.

Nadia heard the smacking of the bodies, fueling her hands to continue their magic on herself. She couldn't hold back anymore and put two fingers in. She squeezed her nipple while thrusting her clit as she groaned louder and louder. Her hands moved faster and faster, mimicking the pace of the couple down the hall.

Tony heard the moans from down the hall and knew very well the origin of them, but disregarded them for now. He was nearing his orgasm and could feel that Monica was closer to it than him. He let go of her neck and bit down hard on it, making Monica split her eyes open. In mere seconds, after Tony kept hitting all her sensitive right spots, Monica fell stiff and squirted all over his cock, her mouth opened wide yet no sound escaped.

Tony thought his cock was about to fall off as he witnessed his partner reaching her orgasm way prior to his, contracting her walls tightly around his cock. His face was filled with an expression of thrill being in control over someone's pleasure.

Tony didn't waste any time, grabbing Monica again, he rolled her onto her back, pulled her legs up and placed them on his shoulders. He glanced at her, whose face was covered by her now-frizzled hair, and saw a look of hunger. He knew that she wanted more.

Meanwhile, Nadia felt pure jealousy as she heard the female companion rushing to another climax.

"Undeserved bitch," she muttered.

But that didn't stop her from nearing her own. Her legs beginning to quiver. She was so close. Her breathing intensified. Her ears were listening with the highest concentration to the other bedroom. She heard Tony moaning louder and louder and knew that he was mere seconds from cumming, and so she picked up the pace, in sync with her employer.

Tony grinded perfectly into Monica, holding her legs tightly as he dominated her creating another rise of moans from the two. He titled slightly forward, stretching Monica out and grabbing her firm tits. Tony groaned and right before commencing his orgasm, he dropped Monica's legs on each side of him. She quickly wrapped around his waist, and then went down, locking her lips in a passion. Tony began to orgasm, his cock contracting powerfully and cumming bucket loads into Monia. Monica rolled her head back, eyes shut and entered her very own world of ecstasy.

Tony then tussled away from Monica, wiped his lips and walked to the bathroom, closing the door behind him. Alone, he glanced at his reflection, analyzing himself and every detail while cooling down. He found it amusing.

Tony blinked, shook his head, and the familiar gaze returned. He smirked. Tony Lombardi was back to normal and it was back to being a mob boss. Opening the door, he leaned against the doorframe and watched Monica snoring. He found her beautiful, angelic-like with her pale complexion. But despite her beauty, he felt nothing towards her. She meant nothing to him besides a memory of pleasure. A memory that will be soon forgotten and by noon tomorrow.

Tony Lombardi knew better than to let his guard down, or worse yet, do something idiotic like starting a family. He was aware, that a family would be his weakness something that he could not afford.

9

SOFIA'S FLIGHT

New York, New York

"Another glass of champagne Madam?" The flight-attendant asked.

This was the fourth time he offered, and Sofia couldn't help but smile at the poor puppy of an old man who was falling victim to an Italian's woman's prestige and charm. Leaning forward, Sofia pretended to have not been able to hear what he said. She used this chance to give the handsome older gentleman a little peek at her large assets. She saw him blush and couldn't help but feel empowered by the effects she placed upon men around her age.

"I would like one now, Grazie."

As soon as the attendant left, she returned her attention to her laptop screen, her eyebrows furrowed as she continued browsing.

Tony Lombardi, the son-in-law, she never met was a shadowy figure. Sofia understood why. After his father, Giovanni had been killed in prison, his son grew up with a chip on his shoulders. Now his hands were in almost every deal spanning across the East Coast and even deep into the Mexican's territory. He was a wild card but was aware to every move made. Like a maestro in chess, he knew everyone's moves before they did. He was smarter than Luca and she needed both of them to consolidate the Italian's grip on New York.

"Here's your glass, madam."

Sofia took the drink, this time disregarding the flight attendant. She was deep in thought as she waved off the man and slowly sipped away.

She swiped across several photos taken of Tony or more like attempts as in every one. His face was either covered by an obstruction because of the angle or his bodyguards were in front of him. She crossed-referenced the features she could pick up from across the databases of several of Harry's intelligence channels, but nothing was found. Tony was a ghost; a man of the radar.

"Old age must be taking a toll on me," Sofia thought while wiping her glasses clean.

If she was successful, then the Giulianis would be

reunited with Lombardis, putting them back in a powerplay against the Saltinottis. It was a risky gamble she was willing to take, not to satisfy herself, but for the family; her late husband and son, Michael and Francesco and late daughter-in-law Jessica Lombardi. It would take her to do whatever to get the family back on top.

To that, the old woman raised her glass and took a long sip.

10

THE MEETING OF GENERATIONS

Manhattan, New York

The restaurant was dead quiet. Besides the staff, who were standing around reserved in each of their corners, there were no customers except one; Tony Lombardi. Classical Italian music was playing in the background and the establishment was popular to Manhattan's Italian residents for over a half-century.

Tony Lombardi was sipping on a glass of red wine while waiting for his dinner companion. He was early by ten minutes, as he usually liked to be, in order to scope out the surroundings. His bodyguards weren't with him which was a sign of respect he offered to his dinner guest that evening.

Tony glanced at his Rolex and calmly took another sip. The time was nearing. He smoothened his tie making sure it looked perfect. It matched his black suit and fit in perfectly with his black leather shoes. Tony hoped his guest would certainly try to at least match his selection of clothing.

Before he could finish his thought, he heard the garcon welcoming a person and directing them over to him. Tony turned and smugly glanced at the old woman who was wearing a black dress, which was hugging her figure tightly showcasing her long-standing curves. The dress was matched her heels. The woman wore a very expensive necklace and it looked fragile.

Tony magnified the way this woman was carrying herself. Sofia was fully aware of her devilish charm and knew how to work it to her advantage. She walked with confidence, but her heart was beating harder than ever.

She saw Tony towering over the table despite being seated. He was too big for his chair. When Sofia came closer, Tony stood up, buttoned up his suit jacket and walked a few steps to Sofia, his hand leading.

"Buona sera, Nonna," Tony said, gazing into the old woman's eyes.

Sofia held his look, returning the same level of intensity and emotion, before speaking. "Ciao, mio nipote."

They shook hands and smiled briefly while their minds already raced with business proposals each wanted to advocate for over the next hour or so.

11

SOFIA DID WHAT? PART 1

Manhattan, New York

Tony couldn't fathom the scene enfolding in front of him. His trousers were below his waist and his cock rose out. It was held by two small old hands, wrapped slowly around it, stroking it. Sofia, his pseudo-grandmother, was on her knees, blessing Tony with the sight of her big bust mature breasts. Sofia looked up at Tony, the passion in her eyes mimicked his. She winked before letting her saliva drip on his cock, making Tony groan.

"My God!"

"Do you like that, grandson?" Sofia said.

Tony nodded, realized he was letting his guard down. He didn't care. He grasped Sofia's head, getting a good grip on her black silky hair and pushed her mouth in. He would stop if Sofia objected but the old woman kept bobbing up and down. She worked it to her advantage knowing her pseudo-grandson's weakness; women.

Sofia couldn't believe the situation she was in. She never imagined being on her knees, sucking another man's cock yet someone two times younger her senior. The only man she was ever with was with her late husband, Michael Guiliani. *Yet, getting the job done meant getting the job done.* With every minute that passed, she became more regretful.

She blamed Luca for the act they found themselves in. *But was it her motherly instincts that kicked in?* Sofia would suck his cock all night if that got the deal done.

Meanwhile, Tony continued enjoying the unimaginable.

* * *

Seventy-two hours ago, Tony didn't know much about his family's roots. He heard of his grandfather, Michael Lombardi, and rival Luca Giuliani but those old days were long over. Sofia talked with Tony about their greatest battles. She then told Tony telling him she had a deal he couldn't refuse. Tony knew that the old woman meant business.

Sofia glance up at him and licked the side of his

cock. She smiled, letting saliva drip slowly from her mouth onto his cock, and then wrapped her large tits around it, causing Tony to moan. She continued giving her son a luscious titjob enjoying the feeling for every whimper, moan and groan she got out of Tony.

Tony couldn't believe the freak this old woman was. He wasn't easily defeated. Sofia had him exactly where she wanted; torturing him. At that thought, he raised up, and eyed Sofia down.

"Get on the bed."

Sofia felt things were going too far fearing she would lose control. In the back of her mind, she couldn't help but do as Tony demanded.

Tony licked his lips as he let his eyes enjoy the sight of the stunning old Italian woman, now completely in the nude and under a dim light. He appreciated the scene, capturing it in his mind, and followed her onto the king-size bed, his arms holding each of her legs and slowly spreading them, revealing her shaven flawless-looking cunt. He admired it for a second, analysed the thickness of the outer lips, its lips' erectness and the level of juiciness it already had.

Tony trailed soft kisses up Sofia's body, paying attention to her sensitive areas and learning her weak spots. They glanced into each eyes, him having inherited the rare shade of green his grandmother gave him. Sofia couldn't help but admit that the things her grandson, Tony, was making her feel were novel and unexperienced. Her late husband, Michael never accomplished such in the their early days of marriage and did not even come close.

Sofia could not afford to be the first to submit. As much as she was enjoying this encounter, she couldn't let herself give in. This was the result from decades of being the wife of the most dangerous mafia family of New York.

Tony knew exactly what Sofia wanted and Sofia inhaled sharply, clenching her hands into fists and grabbing a strong hold of the bed sheets.

It took mere minutes for Sofia to squirm power-fully, scream loudly and shake violently as she reached her orgasm, the first of what would be many to come in the night. Tony didn't expect his grand-mother to be a such a freak, but it turned him on. Sofia Giuliani did not precede her reputation, she owned it.

"What the fuck did you do to me." Sofia gasped, dire for air.

Tony smirked.

"Nothing yet."

Tony spread Sofia's legs again, staring into her eyes intensely. He knew this private encounter was imminent.

Sofia was still trying to catch her breath while she

gazed down, Tony clearly was ready for the next execution.

"No, no—that's enough."

"I'm not done yet, grandmother."

Tony licked her into a level of pleasure she never experienced before. The haziness was overtaking her mind. She then looked down and glared at the cock that was about to enter her. Sofia's old nipples were hard as stone and her cunt was dripping from Tony's dorsum.

Electric waves travelled straight to her spot and her mind began going crazy. When Tony's cock was right against her opening, she pushed him away.

"Wait. What about protection?"

"My women will always accept me in the purest forms, like the day I was born." Tony kissed Sofia. "You, out of all people, should not have any issue with this, capisce?"

Sofia whimpered slightly. She knew that by allowing Tony to enter her, she would become one of his women he had. There was no escape from that title. Their relationship going forward would be in his hands more than hers. She was aware of that from the moment she asked for the meeting, and then again when she agreed to go back to Tony's mansion. He had control, as he always did.

Tony knew he must allow Sofia some level of authority so, he let Sofia ease into the next step. Then, he gripped Sofia's body and began entering her slowly, causing both to groan loudly.

Sofia couldn't believe the size of this young man. He was too big and she was too old and tight. It had been more than twenty years since Don Luca had made love to her before his passing.

It took several attempts from both of them until Tony's shaft settled completely insid. Its mere presence hit all of her sweet spots. She couldn't help but moan loudly at every little thrust, as Tony triggered intense pleasure in its purest form.

Tony grunted heavily, body covered in pearls of sweat as he turned into a creature whose only purpose was to fuck the woman under him.

Mere seconds after, Tony felt Sofia travel into the land of ecstasy as she became limp, losing all control of her limbs and reaching an orgasm, this one was stronger than the previous. She couldn't help but yell loudly, egging her grandson on more. Tony increased his pace, fucking in longer strokes.

"You want it?" Tony said which received him a stone stare from Sofia.

Sofia cursed him for her will for pride was stronger than the satisfaction her body desired. She didn't wait decades for this level of pleasure only to terminate it due to her own foolishness. She then took full control.

"What's wrong, Tony?" She giggled. "Something the

matter?" She spoke softly, her tits squashed in his face causing Tony to moan and groan.

"Oh my fucking god," Tony said, his hands squeezing the incredible mature ass of Sofia, a hand on each cheek and giving it an occasional spanking while she rode him.

"Not bad when an old woman takes charge, huh?"

This was the moment that Tony realised that he wasn't in control anymore. Sofia leaned back up, her hair twirling from the movement and Tony couldn't help but admire the beautiful creation that was Sofia was and is. She placed her hands on his toned upper body and began sensually rising up and down, squeezing his cock tightly getting different moans out from her grandson.

"I'm gonna cum, Mamma," Tony whispered.

That sentence gave Sofia empowerment, making her ride Tony more aggressively. Tony couldn't hold back anymore and without warning, pushed Sofia away, but not enough to detach his tool from her warmness. Tony groaned loudly, and Sofia enjoyed every moment of his weakness.

Tony let everything out, and refused to withdraw from the perfect safe haven until his balls were empty. Sofia gently stroked Tony's head, calming him from the shakes until there were no more.

Minutes passed, Tony laid back and lit a Marlboro.

Sofia sighed. "Is there anything else before we make the deal, my son?"

Tony played with silver streaks of her hair and traced her features with his fingers, enjoying Sofia's soft body. He continued doing so for awhile until he fell asleep, snoring like a drunkard. Sofia then quietly got up, pulled on her clothes and gave Tony a kiss on the cheek.

"Indeed, you are something else, young man." Sofia closed the door gently behind her.

1 2

FAMILY SECRETS

New York City, USA

Vanessa Saltinotti fired up a Marlboro, inhaled deeply and let out puffs of smoke. She began this bad habit only recently, but she learned quite quickly. It surprised her she found a near-full pack inside the living room's sofa. She guessed it had been there for years. She saw her mother and father smoke and the image it portrayed to her was sexy. Vanessa never fathomed how her mother settled for her father, but there was always a reason behind every single one of her mother's moves.

It was close to midnight and the chilly air hardened Vanessa's nipples. She wasn't desperate for her husband, Vincent since this sexual drought had been going on for over three weeks now due to school.

She finished her cigarette, stubbed it out on the frame of the balcony and flicked it over. Going back inside, her mind travelled to her mother's sudden business trip. Usually she would invite her, but by her mother's gesture, she assumed it was more of a private matter.

Vanessa sighed, dropping onto the bed and reaching for her phone. She had dozens of notifications. Being the daughter of mob boss made her popular. Since she was pretty, Vanessa was constantly bombarded with offers to pose in online magazines, social media posts, and even porn sites. She found it humorous in how easy it was to manipulate society when they heard what they wanted, and believed what they liked. Her friends looked up to her, desiring that she pose and ultimately it led her to almost consider it. But she never cared for the materialistic stuff. What Vanessa sought was meaning and purpose through learning law.

Her mind then wandered to her father, so decided to check up on him, His office door was shut, as usual, and she knocked three times before hearing a "Sì?"

"Ciao papà, just wanted to check in to see if you needed anything?"

Vanessa leaned against the doorframe, playing with her hair and her movement causing her tits to bounce a little. Her PINK booty shorts did not leave anything to the imagination.

The moment Jacopo laid eyes on his daughter, he choked on the tea he was sipping and his eyes bulged.

"Sto bene. Per favore lasciami. Ho del lavoro da fare."

Vanessa sighed. *Why is dad acting weird?* "Ok, papà." She pulled the door shut but before she made it back upstairs, Vanessa said, "Papa, where's Mama?"

"In Miami."

"Ok."

* * *

Jacopo's face was sweating bullets, his temperature rising and he was breathing heavy. He glanced down underneath his desk, between his legs, was a Serbian prostitute, licking his cock like a good girl.

Her name was Malina, and she was bought in for five hundred dollars, racking in profits over a grand a night. She was more than worth the cash and the headache that she came with. After the first meeting with Malina, Jacopo knew she was going to get popular really quick. Within a month, she was the most beloved whore around town. Mobsters around town booked nights in advance. There was just something about Malina that made men go crazy.

"Oh Jesus." Jacopo groaned, his head leaning back.

Vanessa heard her father curse but didn't think anything of it as she reached her bedroom. She felt lonely reaching for a cigarette again, then she opened the door to the balcony. She cherished the nice view of New York City from her balcony. She began smoking and thought how bored she was when her mother was not around. Her mother wasn't just Maria, she was her best friend.

"I'm going to Miami to see my mother."

13

FOLLOW HER

New York City, USA

Vincent Romano, the estranged husband of Vanessa Saltinotti, sat in his Cadillac, sipping on vodka from the bottle. Behind the sunglasses, his eyes were bloodshot. He looked way older than his actual twenty five years. In the passenger seat was a brunette. That's all he knew about her and what he called her by. He didn't care for names, as long as she knew who he was and what he could do to her. No further words were needed to get exchanged. After all, Vincent was paying this overpriced whore a grand an hour, so she better be worth it, he thought. He glanced down as she was bobbing on his prick. The way she sucked in her cheeks gave him ultimate pleasure.

Vincent's eyes looked up at the movement of someone. Squinting, he saw the woman he was stalking, dressed in denim shorts, a snug t-shirt, with a suitcase rolling behind her. She looked like the perfect American girl. He saw the suitcase being taken from her by her driver and loaded into the trunk, while she got into the backseat. He forcefully pulled the brunette up, making her scream. Vincent smacked her and pushed her over to the passenger side.

"Where the fuck does this bitch think she's going?"

He gripped the steering wheel.

Julie, the brunette who until up a few seconds ago thought she was pleasing Vincent, was sniffling, holding the side of her face.

As soon as the S-Class sped off, Vincent made a phone call to someone he called the 'The Tracker', a whiz kid that refused to go to Harvard because he thought education was a scam.

"Boss."

"I have a job for you."

"Shoot."

Vincent glanced, the car now barely visible. "I need you to find out where Vanessa Saltinotti is going."

He expected an answer straight away, but when he was met with silence, Vincent was more vexed.

"Are you still fucking there?"

"Yeah, boss. No problem, but do you really want to do that?"

"What the fuck does that mean?"

"I mean, she's a Saltinotti. You know she's untouchable."

Vincent palmed his forehead. "Listen dickhead, she is my wife. I have the fucking right to know where the fuck she is going at all motherfucking times of the day and night. Even how many times her heart beats when she sleeps. Do you fucking hear me?"

There was static on the line. "Hello, hello—"

Vincent hung up, cursing Danny as he started the engine of the Cadillac.

Without looking, he reached for the head of the brunette and pulled it to his lap

"Be quick." Vincent moaned reaching for one of her tits.

14

THE MORNING AFTER...

New York, New York

Tony Lombardi sat at the breakfast table. His legs crossed, sipping on black coffee while watching the local news. Nadia was preparing croissants and chopping up some fruit for a platter. In the background of the white kitchen was Andrea Bocelli, playing his greatest hits.

Tony heard the tapping of footsteps and glanced at the person entering the kitchen. Sofia Giuliani looked gorgeous as she swayed to the table, taking a seat, while smiling at Tony. Her hair was tussled and the top three buttons of her blouse were undone. Her impressive cleavage mesmerized him. His eyes followed the trail of love bites he left on his grandmother, which were dark and visible. Tony smirked, at which Sofia raised an eyebrow and rolled her eyes. Though his staring caused her nipples to poke out.

"Buongiorno!"

"Morning." Sofia said, putting her arms together and teasing Tony with the power of her breasts.

Nadia observed the interesting encounter. Tony had never before allowed one of his nightly playthings to join him for breakfast, never mind even seeing another room except for his, yet here was a very beautiful woman - a few years senior her age - teasing and joking around with him, as if the two knew each other for years. Nadia noted the woman, who was now sitting cross legged, tying her hair in a bun.

"Have whatever is on the table, and if you're not in the mood for that, you can always ask Nadia over there to scramble you whatever you like. She's an incredible chef, if not the best in the world."

Sofia glanced at the woman too, analysing every detail about her. She stood up and walked over to Nadia, extending her hand. "It is an incredible honour to meet you Ms. Nadia."

Nadia, caught slightly off-guard by the greeting, took the woman's hand. "Well, thank you so much, unfortunately I'm not sure whether we met before?"

"I don't think we have, I'm Sofia Giuliani."

At the mention of the name, Nadia's eyes widened.

"You're kidding," Nadia said trying to keep it together. "My apologies for not recognizing you at first, Signora."

Sofia giggled. "Nadia, it's fine, I hope Tony is treating you well I hope."

"You're breaking my balls, Signora." Nadia glanced again at Tony who observed the two women." Yeah, he's a good man."

"Well I'm glad to know that he is appreciated by such." Sofia said.

Nadia blushed still unable to fathom that she was in the same room as the great Sofia Giuliani, the widow of the late Godfather of New York City.

Tony continued sipping on his coffee, his attention elsewhere. He was waiting for a major ruling in New York City's City Council to take place. Depending on their vote, he may needed to take extra measures for handling his business. He sat patiently looking at the TV while the women were engaged in small talk.

"We need to talk," Sofia interrupted Tony deep in his thoughts as she sat down.

She reached for one of his cigarettes, placing it between her lips and began looking for his lighter but to no avail. Tony was quick, pulling out his custom-made Ferrari one from his pocket and flickering it, meeting Sofia's cigarette.

"Okay, but after breakfast. In my office—" Tony said, grabbing a cigarette for himself.

"But what I currently have isn't on the table yet." Sofia said smiling.

"I can serve you perhaps after our little talk."

"We'll see."

"What the hell did I get myself into," both thought as they waited for breakfast to be served.

15

I'VE ARRIVED

Miami, Florida

Vanessa was exhausted from the long flight and couldn't wait to get situated in the hotel, a few blocks away from her mother. She planned on buying Maria a few gifts after catching up on her beauty sleep.

The type of clothes Vanessa had on, got her unwanted attention from the Cuban and Dominicans who looked at her like one of their own while the women looked, obviously jealous. But Vanessa was not bothered in the least, all it would take was one phone call to end the nonsense.

After passing homeland security, where they questioned Vanessa more than anyone, she hurried to the exit looking for a person with a sign that had the name *'Tina Rossi'* written on it. Her parents told her if she ever left outside of New York, to use an alias.

Her chauffeur was young and buff. He smiled as Vanessa approached.

"Ms. Rossi?"

"That's me."

"I'm Matteo and I'll be taking you today. Your mother sent . This way, your luggage is already inside the car."

"Grazie."

They exited the airport.

16

LET'S GET DOWN TO BUSINESS

New York, New York

Tony Lombardi plummeted down on his leather chair behind the wooden desk he had made in Italy, the letters TL were engraved in gold on its side. Sofia Giuliani was in his office, glancing around, reflecting on how it was neater than she expected. There were no papers lying around or ashtrays with buds. She stared at the flat-screen TV with Tony watching the cameras monitor the mansion.

"Tony," Sofia said. "When I came here to meet you, I didn't expect things to go so—" Sofia paused. "So south."

Tony smiled. "The minute you called, old woman, I knew we were going to end up in my bed."

"Oh shut up, I wasn't that easy."

"You weren't, I was just that good." Tony laughed.

Sofia thought before speaking. "I knew exactly what I wanted before I came."

Tony smiled, knowing that he was at that stepping stone a few hours earlier. "Do you mean our love-making or our line of profession?"

Sofia smiled.

"I wonder where you got your charm from," Sofia said.

"Probably from my grandfather, Michael."

"Hmm, I didn't expect that answer."

Sofia reached for a cigarette, lit it and began filling the clean office with smoke. "What do you want to know?"

Tony stood up from his chair, walked around the desk and took Sofia's pack of cigarettes. He pulled one out, his mother held up the lighter for him. He smoked with her, staring into her eyes as she observed his every move.

"Everything about those fucking Saltinottis and Romanos," Tony said midst exhaling.

17

MAKING CONNECTIONS

Upstate New York

"Would you stop with the fucking smoking already? It's dirtying up my car, Nonna," Luca whined, pulling his window down for fresh air.

Sofia Giuliani ignored him as she continued smoking her sweet cigarette, blowing the smoke out into the interior of the 1990 Maybach. A barrier left the pair in the back unseen, with the chauffeur focusing on safely navigating the roads to downtown New York. Sofia admired the city. She remembered the first time she came to New York, and fell in love with its people, buildings and food instantly. She also loved the cold weather. It was one of the reasons she came back.

"Driver, how much longer?" Luca asked.

"Twenty minutes, boss."

Sofia glanced over at her grandson, remembering that his grandfathers were of a tougher calibre and a calmer demeanor than him. His reputation preceded that he was inexperienced and reckless. Sofia could tell by her grandson's hands bawled up and cladding onto his tuxedo trousers, probably hiding his sweaty palms. His face was becoming red. Sofia needed to calm him down, otherwise she would be embarrassed considering the high levels of profiles they will be engaging with.

Sofia took one last drag and then stubbed it in the ashtray. She put her hand on Luca's, grabbing his attention.

"Is there not someone who can help you relax?" Sofia asked.

"Nonna, none of these girls are in my league. They only want one of two things; my money or my cock."

"Grandson, master the first and second will come automatically."

"We have arrived." The chauffeur said with a thick Italian accent, one that Sofia hadn't heard in years.

He got out and opened the door to let our Luca first, who in turn opened the door for his Nonna. Sofia elegantly stepped, grabbing her grandson's hand, smiling to all the flashing cameras while the pair stood in front of the expensive Maybach on a red carpet. They waved and putting her arm into his, the two began walking into the venue.

It was a benefit gala, of the richest and most powerful people around the globe. The attendance list included several world leaders, celebrities and millionaires. However, it was all just a front as the event all hosted the most dangerous criminal figures in the underworld, bringing them together once a year in order to keep peace. It was neutral ground with instruction - *No weapons, attempts and powerplays.*

The celebrities were added into the mix for the media outlets, in order to make the façade more believable. They were just stupid players that none of the big players respected. They were either someone's date or came by invitation.

Sofia and Luca were taken to their table close to the front. The Giuliani family was well known and Sofia appreciated the gesture of respect from the host. When Sofia went to sit, Luca sat first and didn't bother pulling the chair out for her.

"What a shameful act by a young man."

Sofia and Luca turned suddenly.

"I apologize, one of my men should've taken the

initiative and pulled a chair for you, madam." A man spoke with a Russian accent.

"I'm Vladimir Ivanov, host for this evening." He held his hand out for Sofia's.

She brought her hand into to his and the man bowed over, kissing it gently, lingering for a second too long, before standing back upright. "I am Sofia-"

"Giuliani, I am well aware." Vlad cut her off, turning to the man next to her. "And you must be Luca." He shook hands with Luca, his grip hard and tough, before turning his attention back to Sofia, whom grasped for a cigarette and placed it between her lips, looking for her lighter.

Vlad was quicker firing his zippo from his pocket, offering the flame to her. Sofia accepted the gesture.

"It's a pleasure to meet you."

Sofia took a deep drag and exhaled. "The pleasure is all mine."

Luca witnessed the exchange between the two, but did not speak. No matter how powerful the Giuliani family was, their reach was limited to only New York and North Jersey. His criminal organization meant nothing to a man like Vladimir Ivanov.

The Ivanov name was not only honored among the underworld, but was sacred. People that did not respect them were dealt out. Their influence reached far above America.

"I need to speak to a few other guests, please do let me know if you two need anything." Vladimir extended his courtesy to be extended to both, his eyes still glued to Mrs. Giuliani.

Sofia smoked. "What a character," she muttered as she gazed at the stage in front of them.

But as Luca looked into her eyes, he could see that his grandmother was up to something.

"Tell me, Nonna. Why is he more important to you than us Italians?"

"Grandson, he's just a pawn in the game. I have things under control. Just be patient."

* * *

The night dragged on, live jazz was being played by bands, and people were networking. Sofia and Luca came with a precise plan to execute. They needed a connection through Europe to extend their business and power. As long as they dealt with the right people, a mafia war could be avoided.

Sofia turned away from the couple her and Luca were engaged in a conversation with and went over to a balcony that oversaw all of New York, its bright lights shimmering. She enjoyed the view, a glass of champagne in hand. It was cold, as she forgot her jacket inside.

"A bit chilly out here, isn't it?"

Sofia turned and stared up at the icy eyes of Vladimir Ivanov, holding his jacket out and offering it to her. She allowed him to slip it on and continued gazing at the distance.

"You've hosted the evening very well so far, Mr. Ivanov."

"Vlad for you, Mrs. Giuliani."

Sofia turned. "Then it's Sofia for you."

The two stood in silence for a while. It was their little escape from the craziness orbiting inside.

"You came here for a reason, Donna."

"Wouldn't that be a question from my late husband?" She replied.

Vladimir shook his head, a smile plastered on his face; a face that is worthy of the nickname, "Ice King".

"Me and you both know who really controls the future of the Giuliani family," Vladimir said.

Sofia had no intention to bow down to the Ice King.

"I want a distributor in the East."

Sofia continued smoking, exhalin into the cold air.

"Just a distributor? Or a connection?"

Sofia looked up to him, cigarette still in hand and casually smoking, blowing it into his face.

"That depends."

Vladimir smiled. "On?"

"Whether you—do business with widows."

Vladimir grabbed Sofia's ass with a strength that made her feel like a plaything. She could feel him becoming harder and his cock rubbed against her leg, making her gasp.

"I think we have an agreement."

18

THE RUSSIANS?

Upstate New York

"So, we're dealing with the Russians now?" Luca said looking at Sofia sitting opposite him, whom had a dreamy look on her face. Luca heard all of the horror stories of the Ivanov's. They were a family of savages, ruthless and rotten to the core. Luca knew that Vladimir must be taken out.

"Grandson, we must continue to have them in the picture if we want to expand."

"Nonna, he must go. Ever since Jacopo took over, Vladimir has taken even more of New York. I can't let this go on any longer."

Luca sighed, scratching his forehead. This arrangement had already complicated several of his operations in Manhattan as well as the territories under the Ivanov's power he had planned to hit. He glanced at his mother again, who was in her own world smoking a cigarette, and wondered whether the agreement that was made with Vladimir all those years ago was still effective since the Saltinottis were still in control.

"Don't do anything stupid, Grandson. We don't want an all-out war. Not now."

"We still haven't even dealt with Jacopo. Now this, Nonna."

Luca laid back on the leather sofa, his cigarette almost finished, while his mind devised a plan. One that would cost a lot of business for the Saltinottis and could perhaps even cripple them. It was a question of etiquette, whether to execute it or to leave everything as it was. That would mean keeping his grandmother happy. But on the other hand, he was Luca Giuliani, Luca Lombardi; son of both of most feared mob bosses of New York City. He needed to make a choice, but for now, he chose to listen.

19

MARIA'S HAREM

Miami, Florida

Maria Saltinotti moaned loudly at her gigolo's thrusts, spreading her to his raging cock. They were in her hotel room's large shower, a warm stream of water both bodies, flowing over their aggressive make-out session. The man positioned his hand on the shower wall for balance, thrusting into her as deep as he could, until he met resistance, and then withdrew entirely leaving only the tip trapped between Maria's puffy lips. Giving it a second, he then thrusted hard into her. He did this repeatedly, causing Maria to scream.

Her legs were shaky and weak. She could barely keep herself up as the man violently fucked her from behind, causing their bodies to smack loudly and echoing through the shower. Both hands of her hands were placed on the walls with the side of her face pressed against her hands. Maria was too gobsmacked to even thrust backwards as the man drained the soul out of her.

The man slapped the Maria's firm ass, giving her consecutive spankings and grabbing a cheek strongly, continued his backshots. It didn't take long for Maria to reach an orgasm. She closed her eyes, mouth wide open yet no scream escaped her lips. The man didn't stop seeking his own finish.

He turned Maria around, reached for her legs and picked her up. With one hand, he grabbed his thick tool, lined it up along her opening and entered Maria again, moaning loudly, his eyes closed. She was tighter than anyone he ever fucked, felt better and was able to handle more of him than anyone in his past.

Maria loved the way the man played rough with her, the way he handled her, like a savage. Like a true man. The man grunted but kept his attack up. He first felt the burn in his cock, then the twitch, followed by the rise of his cum erupting and covering the walls of Mrs. Saltinotti. The man didn't know whether she was on birth control or the morning after pill, but at this stage of time he could not care less.

He grabbed Maria's neck, forcing her to look up at

him, and then passionately kissed her with a hunger she had never felt before. She cried out from the pleasurable pain inflicted and grabbed the back of the man's head, pulling his hair tightly.

They shared a passionate look with each other, acknowledging the power of the other. He loosened his grip, and let Maria slowly down, his eyes never leaving hers.

The man felt proud watching his art. It turned him on again and his cock did not hesitate to express its own life again as it swiftly hardened.

Maria's eyes bulged as she saw his large cock rise from the dead, transforming into the familiar beast she thought had tamed couple minutes prior. 'You've got to be kidding me.' She thought and looked back at the man's face, who was smiling.

"On your knees."

Maria lowered herself. The man pressed a button to his left and reduced the pressure of the water to accommodate as Mrs. Salinotti got comfortable. He pulled her hair into a ponytail, assuring it wouldn't get into the way of his pleasure.

Mari touched his raging dick, which twitched wildly in anticipation. Now that she was right in front of it, it seemed even bigger. Her tiny hand did not fit around it, and she couldn't help but giggle at the humor of this. She began stroking it slowly.

Stroking away from the tip, Maria held the grip tightly and gave the man's tip a linger kiss, teasing it a little by licking it. She heard him curse under his breath and smiled up at him, giving the underside of his cock a long lick.

"Stop fucking teasing me," the man moaned, holding her hair tighter.

At his command, Maria slipped his raging tool past her lips and began sucking the life out of it, bobbing on it, her left hand playing with his big balls.

The man lost all sense of rationale as he witnessed his client on her knees, blessing him with her incredibly skilled mouth. Maria knew exactly what spots to go for as he felt his balls burning from desire for an orgasm. He glanced down at her and made eye contact with Maria, who smiled before deepthroating his entire cock.

"Sweet Mary," the man cursed.

Maria continued bobbing, taking all of it and sucking harder. She increased her pace and intensified the blowjob. The man had no possible chance to hold back and moaned, his cock beginning to contract out of control. He withdrew it from Maria's mouth just in time before exploding, his cum splattering across Maria's face, unloading every drip of it onto her, not leaving a blank spot.

The man looked at his work and smiled. Maria was

completely in shock at the amount he came. The man grabbed his cock and rubbed it against Maria's lips, who gave him access to her mouth again.

"You are something else," Maria said, looking up at the man.

A ringing of a phone interrupted their moment. Maria stumbled while trying to get the phone, keeping her eyes on the gigolo's. Without glancing at the caller ID, she picked up.

"Si."

"Maria Saltinotti, we have your daughter. Listen up or she dies."

2 0

MY DAUGHTER IS…

Miami, Florida

The gigolo watched his client cry, until she touched her chest and felt short of breath. One minute, she was smiling, and the next, she was broken down in front of her boy toy.

The man wrapped his arms around Maria, hugging her close to his hard frame. Even at this very moment, he tried to sympathize with the old woman.

"Vladimir, Oh my God! They—"

"Shh," the man said. "Whatever it is, you'll take care of it."

"What? I'll take care of it? What good are you Russians for?" Maria got up, put on her bathrobe and lit up a cigarette.

"Get out—get out now! Here's your money." Maria tossed a few hundred dollar bills at the man. "Hurry, I need to call my husband. Our daughter has been kidnapped."

"Ok but are you—"

"Si, Puta. Now go."

* * *

Maria's world collapsed in mere seconds. Her body was trembling from fear. The worry too heavy on her shoulders, perhaps heavier than her crown. The Mafia Queen was experiencing a repeat of history. This happened to her once and the first time, she didn't see her first child for over twenty years. Then one day, he was found in one New York's trash trucks.

The Saltinotti family was not one to fuck with. Whoever fucked with them had some serious balls they were willing to lose.

Maria got up, clenching her fists and she stared at the door. She didn't want to call Jacopo. She already knew that once war began, the blood will flood New York's streets until everyone would be wiped out.

Instead, she called a familiar foe; Tony Lombardi. *How odd!*

"Hello, I need a favor, Tony."

"Who is this?"

"Maria Saltinotti."

"What the fuck are doing calling me?"

"My daughter has been kidnapped. I need your men in Miami to find her. I'll take care of you. Don't worry. Please do it quietly."

"Where was Vanessa?"

"I don't know—I don't know."

"You want to start a war with the Cubans," Tony giggled, "You know what they say about not being able to fight your own battles?"

"I will make those fucks remember this until the end of their lives, I want every single cocksucker who took my daughter to remember that they were the reason their entire bloodline was killed, chopped away like the meaningless dirt of this ear that they are. That is what I want them to remember. So you're either in, or out."

"Well, said."

"If you don't stand with me Tony, I will make sure you will forever be an enemy of my family."

"Aren't we already so?"

"Don't fuck with me, Tony. I know you very well."

Tony was amused. He had been sitting on the edge of the bed, listening to this old woman after just getting finished fucking the brains out of one of his whores who sound asleep. Now, a Saltinotti was threatening his organization.

"Mmm. So, someone is fucking with your family and that makes them my problem."

"Si. And remember that night we spent together. If you want that again, you'll help me."

Tony shook his head remembering it all too and well.

"Ok, I'll send my men out but don't you ever threaten me again, capisce?"

"Ok, Tony. I'm sorry. I'm just a nervous wreck. If Jacopo finds out—"

"He won't. I'm on it."

The line was cut.

* * *

Tony put on his boxers and stepped out of his bedroom, treading down the spiral staircase and entering the kitchen.

Nadia perked up at her boss.

Tony said, "I need you to take care of the girl upstairs for a few days. I want her again when I come home." He grabbed a glass of water and took a sip. "She's not feeling well and there are a few things I need to take care of."

"Of course, boss. Are you ok?"

Tony gulped down the rest of his glass. "You won't be able to reach me for a day or so. I'm taking care of something in Florida and I will call you once everything is over," he said while dialing Ray Gallagher.

Nadia nodded, observing Tony Lombardi giving specific instructions over the phone. Her nipples began to harden when she saw Tony's cock bulge out his robe. *The things I'd do to my boss,* she thought almost forgetting herself.

* * *

Tony hung up on Ray, sighed, and left Nadia in the kitchen.

He jumped in the shower, got dressed and when he was ready to leave, he stopped in the doorframe and glanced over his shoulder one last time.

"Will you comeback safely?"

Tony glanced at Nadia seeing the fear in her eyes. "I always do, this time it's no different."

21

WHODUNNIT?

South Beach, Miami

"Ray, talk to me," Tony said over the phone.

"I can't find the Saltinotti girl, Tony. It's weird, there's nothing on her ever leaving New York. It's like she fucking disappeared."

"What the hell are you saying then?"

"I'm saying, we don't know where she is. My men in the precincts have been working day and night on this. They got families, Tony."

"For Christ's sake, you're supposed to be able to handle these things, you know?" Tony said lighting up a cigarette. "God! I just got an idea!"

"What is it, Tony?"

"Her husband Vincent. He might be in on it."

"Yeah, that wouldn't surprise me, Tony."

"Ray, have your boys check in on Vincent Romano."

"Ok!"

"Hurry. I need this done. Her fucking mother's getting on my nerves."

"You're still fucking her, huh?"

"I gotta go."

* * *

An hour later

"Got a lead, Boss."

"Shoot."

"Castle Beach, #147. It's a villa in South Beach."

"I'll be there in a few minutes. Good job, Ray."

* * *

"You two, stay right here," Tony said to his men.

A red Ferrari was parked outside Villa #147. The expensive car was garnering a lot of attention.

"Whoever took Vanessa is a fucking amateur," Tony thought.

Tony was on his way to #147 when a young man rushed by him with a pizza, irritating Tony.

"Hey, kid. That's mine. I'll take it."

"$10.99 sir."

"Keep the change." Tony gave the boy a hundred-dollar bill.

"Wow, sir. Thanks."

"Run on."

The boy went downstairs, staring at the Ferrari, then to Tony's men in black suits.

"Delivery for Room 147," Tony said fixing himself and hiding his gun underneath the pizza box.

No one came.

Then, he pressed the bell.

Moments later, a fat man opened the door in boxers, tank top and a robe.

"Motherfucker."

Tony laughed. "C'mon, let's have a talk, Freddo."

Freddo lowered his shoulders. "I didn't do anything Tony. I swear."

"That's not the complete truth, is it now?" Tony shut the door behind them and followed Freddo into the kitchen.

"Hands behind your head. No funny stuff or else."

Dirty dishes were piled up and the brown recliners matched the color of the carpet, as if being sucked in.

"So you still haven't redecorated your grandma's place, huh?"

"Why would I, it's vintage."

"More like a dump," Tony said.

Freddo sat while Tony stood up.

"Freddo, I'm going to ask you once. If I'm not satisfied with your answer, you'll be saying goodnight."

"Tony, I'll tell you whatever you want to know. Please don't kill me."

"That depends. Now, I need to know if someone has recently asked you for a job."

"You know I can't talk about the shit I do for my clients, Tony."

Tony held his hand up. "Let me finish." He looked at his pistol. "Someone dear to me got snatched up here earlier." Tony lit up a cigarette and gazed at Freddo.

"Tony—"

"Don't be a wiseguy. I need answers. Who's behind it?"

"I don't know, Tony—"

"Is it Vincent Romano? Because if I find out you are in this shit, I'll slice both of your heads off starting with you."

"Ok, Tony. It was him. He told us to get her but it has nothing to do with the family."

"I'll be the judge of that. Give me a location."

"I don't have one, Tony."

"You're pissing me off."

"He's—he's back in New York now with Vanessa."

Tony nodded, grabbing Freddo's shoulder. "I won't forget this my friend."

Tony shot him once in the head and the fat man dropped to the floor. Seconds later, Tony stepped out of the villa and went back downstairs.

"Chop up the body and toss it in the river. I'll be in the car."

"Ok, Boss."

Two hours passed and Tony flew out of Miami with more purpose than he initially walked in with. A target in his head. His fingers were trembling— his Beretta was shaking. A war was coming, and he will be the initiator of its wrath and chaos. Freddo was a made man.

YOU DID WHAT?

Manhattan, New York

Vincent Romano downed shot after shot of vodka, not giving a fuck about his father's anger simmering from the corner of his office. They were inside the mansion and the door was closed.

"I didn't think I'd raise an idiot, but it appears I have," Don Johnny Romano said.

His voice was calm, levelled, and precise. Vincent knew very well that there was his father's rage was coming and it was only moments away. He poured himself another glass, filling it to the brim and inhaling it.

"Pa, I did the right thing."

"No, you fucking never do," Don Johnny yelled.

Here we go again!

"Do you know that you fucked up any sort of alliance between us and the Saltinottis? You fucking kidnapped your own goddamn wife. Jacopo will have our heads." The Don palmed his face. "And Maria, Jesus Christ, what am I to tell her?"

Vincent grimaced. *He never anticipated seeing his father as a weak person. And to think that once upon a time the Romano family used to be feared. Others asked for their blessing before doing any move. Now they were all in shambles and the Saltinottis are running them.*

"Pa, I'll fucking handle it—" Vincent was interrupted by a knock on the door. "Who the fuck is it? Don't you know we're talking business?"

The door creaked, and Lucia, Vincent's sister came smiling nervously.

"I'm sorry to disturb—the boys. Mamma sent me. She was wondering if you want me to bring dinner?"

Vincent studied the cleavage Lucia's top was providing, his eyes were glued to the sight for several seconds as his cock got hard.

That's Lucia! No fucking way!

"Sure, miele," Don Johnny said. "We have nothing further to discuss." Johnny looked at his son, still disappointed.

"Okay, I was also wondering—" Lucia stepped

further inside, playing with her fingers. "Could I go out with my friends, Papà? We want to catch a movie and then hit the arcade."

Sneaky bitch!

"Sure you can go sweetheart. Be careful, and hey—" Don Johnny held up his finger. "Write the address down on the refrigerator and let Antonio drive you, capsice?"

"Capisce, Papà. Grazie!" Lucia smiled. "You're the best." And just like that, Lucia sprung out of the room, shutting the door behind her.

Vincent turned to his father. "I'll deal with the Saltinottis."

"Last time I checked, I'm still the Don, figlio."

"Not for long, Papà. You're retiring soon."

Don Johnny Romano shook his head. "You fucking little shit," he muttered as the door closed.

23

PIZZA TIME

Little Italy, Brooklyn-New York

Tony was glancing at the many kinds of pizza through the shop's glass. The place was stuffy and Tony sensed that the air conditioning was out of order. He pulled on his collar, loosening his tie and met the eyes of who appeared to be the owner of this little place.

"Double pepperoni and cheese, signor," Tony said looking back at the car waiting for him outside. "Make it two extra-large."

The owner nodded and went to pick out the slices. After heating them, he put each slice in a box and handed them to Tony.

"Keep the change."

"Grazie, signor," The old man said holding a hundred-dollar bill.

The door was opened to today's car, a Maserati Quattroporte, and Tony was grateful for its AC. He leaned back in his seat and wiped the sweat off his face. The weather today was extremely hot and humid in the 90s. Tony took off his suit jacket, placing it beside him and opened the top button of his shirt, letting his tie down.

The glass between him and the driver lowered and the face of Tony's driver appeared in the mirror. "To where now, Boss?"

"Just take me back to the Baccarat, Paul. Take this, they say it's the best pizza in New York. It says outside that this place was found in the 1960s.

Paul chuckled. "Grazie, Boss." Paul took the box through the window. "You know, Boss, this place has only been open for 2 years?"

Tony sighed glancing out the window to the pizza shop. He saw the owner behind the till, looking out for the next customer.

"Fucking sharpie."

Paul chuckled as the two men bit into their slices at the same time.

"Greasy piece of shit," Tony said.

"Yeah, Boss."

"Let's go."

"Ok, Boss." Paul sped off moments later.

24

FINDING VANESSA

Manhattan, New York

Traffic was a nightmare. Drivers passed wherever they could, no regard to lanes or others. The street lights were their bibles and Tony didn't know why he was surprised.

He had finished his slice, tossing the crust back into the box and closing it, dropping it next to his legs. He reached for a tin box inside his suit jacket and fondled a cigarette out, lighting it. He smoked, enjoying every breath dirtied with smoke. Then, there was the exhale, of smoke surrounding him. It was art, an act of class that survived time, forever part of history.

It took them 90 minutes until they reached the

Baccarat Hotel. A valet opened the door and Tony stepped out, slipping him a few notes of cash.

A shiny marble covered the entrance leading up to the reception area, behind which two beautiful women stood. What Tony liked about this place was that not many had access to it; prices were the highest in town and it was not suited for families.

Tony nodded to the receptionist, who briefly glanced at him then back to the elderly man she was serving. Waiting for a lead from Ray, he checked his phone. *No message. What the fuck is Ray doing?*

The interior of the elevator lit up in sapphire and the floor was color in a sparkly gold, as was the ceiling. Tony pressed the button for the TY Warner Penthouse on the top floor and the black display flashed red. Tony swiped his key card and the flashing turned into green and the doors closed shut.

* * *

Vivaldi was playing in the background, at a sensible volume. Tony toyed with his cigarette bud, rolling it between his fingers. He wasn't nervous. He had come here with one move in mind; one play that he was certain will bring the Saltinottis to their knees. If the message he was so waiting for wouldn't give him what he was looking for than he must improvise.

The doors glided against the wheels and opened, the reception of a penthouse emerged. Tony palmed his forehead and entered. He threw his jacket over the leather chair's arm of a leather chair. His hand went through the thickness of his hair, pulling it back, and he fixed himself a cold whiskey. He sipped on the alcohol, feeling it flush his system, and gazed out the windows viewing an incredible view of the skyscrapers that landmarked New York City. There was beauty among the chaos. That was New York City.

Tony's phone vibration interrupted his thoughts. He reached and read the message. It took him mere seconds to skim it and when he reached the final period, he chuckled. Holding up the glass up, he smiled devilish.

"Cheers to you, New York, the Big Apple of fucking opportunities." He clanked the glass against the window and downed his drink.

The clock struck nine. It was a Saturday night, people were out and the streets were experiencing a flooding of alcoholics ready to club all night long, until the break of dawn. From underpaid teachers to underage students, from loners to jocks, rich to poor, Saturday night did not discriminate.

Tony had changed into a black suit, and blue shirt, tucked in and unbuttoned enough to allow a peek at his inked chest; a verse from the Bible.

His black hair was slicked back and he looked his age of twenty-something year old. He looked and smelled expensive. He slipped his gold ring on, an Omega around his wrist and the tin box of expensive cigarettes on the inner pocket of his jacket. Not forgetting the most important part - the unmarked Beretta. That gun was responsible for the deaths of countless men and Tony Lombardi had always treasured it.

He called for the lift and while doing so, sent a text message to Paul, his driver. The ride down was far quicker than the ride up. He stepped through the luxurious lobby, two new ladies were now behind the desk, their eyes admiring Tony Lombardi.

"Where to Boss?"

"Rompus Room," Tony said, glancing out the window and placing his chin on his palm.

No reply from Paul, the tinted glass lifted and taciturnity overtook the atmosphere of tonight's wheels; a black Hummer with bulletproof windows. The car was not registered and Tony did not care. It was the least of his worries.

The Hummer quickly approached, despite the heavy traffic in downtown Manhattan, New York, *the city that never sleeps.*

During the ride, Tony daydreamed about relocating downtown to expand his operations.

Wildly, he pictured what it would be like to stay in the same place as Sofia Giuliani - the endless opportunities that came with such an idea. Perhaps they could arrange for weekend getaways. Somewhere close to nature where they would become animals themselves. He pictured her naked mature body, slightly covered by a duvet but most of her petite rear visible. The sun sneaking through the blinds and birds twitching. He would cuddle up to the old woman, turn her over and wake her up with his tongue. He would suck her old cunt a million times until she came, gripping his hair, moving to the length of his tongue, moaning his name out loud. And then he would pull himself up, to face his psuedo-grandmother, feeling her old tiny hands guiding his cock into the deepest part of her - welcoming him. Tony would—

"Boss, we've arrived."

Tony looked at the qqueue waiting outside the Rompus, dressed in all sorts of crazy clothes. The SUV stopped in front of the VIP section and a club bouncer opened the door.

"How many?"

"Just me." Tony replied.

The bouncer nodded and shut the door, leading Tony straight past the VIP gate. Tony didn't get checked and was ushered right inside.

* * *

Spanning across two floors, the Rompus was divided into two; the dance floor and an area that was for the more of elite. New York's moneybags were gathered there and the sexiest girls who sought their attention, looking to be picked up.

Several moneybags were sitting, some danced with the babes to the music. Waitresses were walking up and down, between tables, bringing food and drinks.

Tony leaned against the bar catching the attention of the bartender. "What can I get you?"

"A place," Tony said swiftly.

"A place? Never heard of such a beverage. How do you mix it, I can try make it for ya?"

"The place where I can find Vincent Romano." Tony stared at the big man with huge arms. Tony guessed he was an American football player in the past. From the crookedness of the man's nose, he also had a history of fights.

"Don't know nobody called that."

Tony smiled. "Charlie, Charlie, Charlie." He shook

his head. "Let me tell you how this will go down." Tony lit a cigarette and inhaled deeply. "I will tell you about yourself, that you are Charlie Hernandez, former football player who got cut after suffering a knee injury that never healed. Not even your poor mother and grandmother knew what kinda shithole you vanished into after you stop playing." Tony paused, exhaling. The bartender's face turned red. He wanted to fight. Tony continued, "Must've been hard though," Tony's eyes leveled a cold stare at the big man. "Being the reason your grandmother died in that crack house."

"Fucking son of a bitch!" Charlie swung but Tony had got out of the way, before pulling out his Beretta and sliding it just over the tip of the counter.

"Now let's start again and you better be smart, this time. Tell me what I need to know or it'll be your mother next."

Charlie's eyes widened.

"Okay, okay. That guy comes around midnight with a chic who usually picks up a guy from the VIP. She then goes home with him for an hour or two. Vincent waits here for her to come back before the victim wakes up finding his credit cards and cash stolen."

Tony let go of Charlie, slipping his gun into the holster and stepped away. "Double shot of Whiskey on the house." Tony said pulling out a cigarette.

"God damn! Motherfucker, I have to pay for that," Charlie said.

"It's not my problem."

Charlie turned to get Tony's drink.

* * *

Tony Lombardi waited patiently by the window sill. He swirled the contents of his glass casually and looked outside to the street. He was deep in concentration when a few loud female voices travelled across the lounge. He turned, seeing three girls in tight dresses showing the curves of their asses, giggling and gossiping. They were making a scene. They made sure that everyone noticed them hoping someone would buy them drinks. Tony turned again and continued looking out the window.

He continued imagining the moves Vincent might make- the ones if he had the balls to do.

"Why are you here if you are going to only stare out the window?" a young woman said.

Tony came back to reality. The voice was soft with authority. It was Vanessa Saltinotti in the reflection of the window. He studied her for a second, his eyes rolling over her features, including her big brown eyes, pale upper-chest and busty cleavage she was teasing to everyone in the room. Her legs and her posture was one of strength. She knew how to carry herself, probably the result of a sport she was an avid participant in since a very young age.

"You can be in a room full of people but sometimes your own company trumps everyone's in the room. I heard you were missing."

Vanessa rolled her eyes. "Vincent kidnapped me again. I want to get out of here before he comes back with one of his whores," she said taking a seat, crossing her legs.

Tony turned around and met her eyes. Her brunette hair indicated a rebellious nature and the 6-inch sex-heels she had on confirmed a slutty trait. As soon as Tony met her glance, he saw Vanessa blushing. She had no chance from the very beginning.

Tony Lombardi continued playing the victim telling her that her mother called him in the middle of a big deal to come to Miami to find her. His conversation was dominating Vanessa's and it wasn't long until the pair were making out furiously in the backseat of the Hummer. Paul navigated the car around the busy streets of the Manhattan.

Tony held Lucia by her throat, gathered her long hair into a fistful and brought her head down onto his cock.

"Fuck, I've never had one this big." Vanessa muttered before opening her mouth and licking.

Tony forced the pretty mouth of Vanessa down his cock, feeling the back of her mouth and entering her throat. She gagged and he nearly came inside it. "Damn," Tony said.

Vanessa's eyes twinkled as they met Tony's. She smiled, releasing his cock out of her mouth and slapped it across her face. "You haven't seen anything yet." She teased, deep throating Tony once again, while he was holding her hair in a ponytail.

He pulled on it and Vanessa came back up. He kissed her fiercely, and firmly ripped her dress down to expose her tits. C-cup's and they were - a handful, Tony thought as he squeezed them, biting Vanessa's neck and moving his other hand down between her legs. She opened her legs. Before the two could go any further, the car stop and it was time to get out.

Tony slipped his cock back in and took his jacket off, putting it on Vanessa's shoulders so her tits wouldn't be exposed. They hopped out, hands entangled. Tony looked back noticing a black wagon parked on the opposite of the street. They swiftly entered the lobby to the lifts. The wait seemed to take an eternity. Tony held her hand, pushing Vanessa in front of him knowing exactly she wanted to do.

The lift came and they entered. Tony swiped the key card once and pressed the button for the 45th floor. Before the doors closed, Tony glanced at the receptionist, who behind her spectacles was looking at the pair, her mouth agape and somehow Tony could sense she was turned on by their act.

He smiled and winked at the young woman until the doors completely shut, and then Vanessa was all over him again. Despite the 6-inch heels, she wasn't even close to his huge frame. Tony bent down a little to meet her lips. Irritated at the fact, he grabbed Vanessa by her thighs and easily lifted her. She wrapped her legs around his waist, her arms around his neck and embracing his tongue.

Tony carried Vanessa across his suite, into his king sized bed and dropped her gently. They stared at each other, knowing full well that the night had only just began.

* * *

Tony unbuttoned his shirt slowly, watching Vanessa getting turned by the number of buttons being popped. He smiled at her lustful and horny face she had put on. Perhaps this was a reminder of Vanessa's young age, being only 24. She was sheltered away from the world and this was her personal mission on getting her life back. She had a lot to learn, Tony thought, but that wasn't his problem. She chose to be ignorant and self-absorbed instead of realizing the predicament her family was in, or the actions that put them there.

Tony tore the rest of the buttons but left on his trousers. He kicked his shoes off and before Vanessa could reach the laces of her heels, Tony grabbed her feet and slowly removed them. It was all part of the act. Once the second heel came off, he threw it over his shoulder and his hands went to her legs, moving upward. He pulled Vanessa's dress up, inching it just above her ass. Tony's hands then went to the edges of her panties and he smiled. He bent down and sucked on her nipple, causing Vanessa to moan. He then quickly pulled her panties down and tossed them over his shoulder.

"Get up."

"Why?"

"Because I said so. Turn around." He said watching Vanessa do so obediently.

Tony reached for her zipper and slowly pulled it down, kissing her skin along the unwinding trail of the metal brackets. Her dress dropped. Turning around, Vanessa exposed her big tits to him, then she wrapped her arms around him. She went to fiddle with Tony's belt and then his zipper until there was nothing but cock—a large one.

Tony slapped Vanessa's ass and squeezed it firmly. Then he pushed against her until her knees reached the edge of the bed causing Vanessa to stumble downward. She looked beautiful. Her pale skin contrasted the dark sheets. Her legs were timidly together and her arms crossing her nipples and big breasts. *Who was she covering up for?*

* * *

A few hours after their lovemaking session, Vanessa said lighting up on Tony's cigarettes, "Damn! No one, not even Vincent has fucked me so good before, and I really mean no one."

Tony smiled. "And no one ever will again." He stated, caressing her chin and cheek.

Tony then got up and went out on the balcony, having a smoke. He welcomed the harsh taste and inhaled sharply. He found himself attracted to the city lights. There was a certain allure to it. Perhaps it was tempting him to stay.

He finished his cigarette and went inside again. Glancing towards the bed, Vanessa Saltinotti was sleeping deeply. The bed sheet covered up to her chest, her tits were on full display for Tony to enjoy.

Pretty, he thought. *Vanessa needs to stop being gullible and grow up. No more careless nights out. She was smart, but didn't think ten steps ahead. She wouldn't make it far in Tony's criminal underworld, but perhaps she'll be a successful marketing director, or something similarly trivial.* Tony knew she was Jacopo's favorite daughter. Hence, he went so far to fuck his little sweetheart so viciously. This was Sofia and Tony's move.

Looking up at the camera in the ceiling, Tony smiled, his eyes were twinkling. He pulled his hand up next to the ear making a phone gesture, "Call me." The Romanos and Saltinottis would be outraged to find Jacopo's precious daughter with a Lombardi.

25
THE SETUP

Downtown Manhattan

The camera's footage in Tony's penthouse was clear and was not restricted only to the first encounter of that night, instead it contained more than 12 hours. Tony and Vanessa continued fucking, sleeping some hours and fucking the rest. Room service in the morning and for lunch, left their meals outside the door often hearing the couple's moans.

Tony sat up in the bed midday. Completely naked, he pulled the cover aside, stepped out of the bed and headed to the source of noise in his place.

What welcomed him was sight of the young brunette, on tip-toes, navigating around the kitchen clanking pans together and all sorts of things?

Vanessa *Saltinotti was clearly out of her mind*, Tony thought while leaning against the door and observing the daughter of the great Don Jacopo Saltinotti. She was wearing pink panties and Tony was already imagining a repeat of events.

He treaded lightly, his eyes settled on Vanessa, watching her expressions while closing in on her, until her face snapped up and saw Tony.

"Good afternoon, handsome," Vanessa said blushing and tucking her hair behind her ear.

Tony didn't bother replying. He was focused on another matter as he closed in on her.

Vanessa was trying her hardest to ignore him, her brown eyes stuck on the pan frying eggs, her back turned to Tony. His scent hardened her nipples as pictures conveying their fucking and tossing in the bed next door flooded her mind.

Tony placed both hands on either side of Vanessa, diving his nose into the messy brunette's hair and took a deep breath. His blood was rushing to his thick member and slowly coming to life. He moved Vanessa's hair away from the nape of her neck and began kissing it, slipping another hand around to her front and palming one of her tits. He squeezed it hearing Vanessa take a sharp intake of air, leaning back into Tony.

Without anything further, Tony took a step back, gripped her right leg and raised it along the kitchen top.

Pulling her panties aside, he entered Vanessa in one long stroke.

"Fuck Tony!"

For the next ten minutes, the only sounds in the room were the fucking noises and moans. The eggs were starting to stick and burn.

Vanessa's cunt was overflowing with juices, Tony's cock was creamed up. Vanessa couldn't help herself, with the uncontrolled groans. It felt so good and she was about to come. Tony increased his pace, fucking Vanessa savagely, her moans music to his ears.

It wasn't long until she was forced to pull away from Tony's tool, not able to take any more, her eyes rolled back into her head.

Tony turned Vanessa around and lifted her onto the counter, spreading her legs and getting between them, fucking her again. It was incredible. Not once did Tony slow down.

Tony's cock was fighting for space every time it entered. He couldn't keep cool anymore and his strokes burst with more power. Vanessa sensed he was coming and held her legs around him tighter, allowing no room for him to escape her insatiable g-spot. A few more strokes and Tony exploded inside Vanessa.

Breathing heavily, Tony pulled his face into Lucia's neck, catching his breath.

"You're something else, Tony Lombardi."

"I know."

Vanessa went back to cooking as the phone rang in Tony's bedroom.

Tony walked in and answered, not recognizing the caller-ID.

"Lombardi, You motherfucker!"

Tony smirked, recognizing the voice. "Put your father on the phone, Vanessa's husband, Vincent Romano."

"You fucked up, Tony. You fucked with the son of a made-man."

"Who the fuck do you think you are, you dirty piece of shit? I'll skin you and fucking hang your skeleton up in the fucking museum downtown—" Tony snapped.

The phone hung up.

Tony sighed waiting for the phone to ring again. It didn't take long. This time, Don Johnny Romano was on the other line, a voice with more reason despite anger lurking in the back.

"Who are you?" The Don spoke calmly.

Tony chuckled. "What are you doing talking to one of your rivals and you have no idea who you are talking to."

"You are testing my patience, which you should be grateful for. I can have you whacked right now, so you better talk fast, what do you want?"

"For you to pay for our business," Tony stated ending the call. He switched the ringer off it and ignoring the incoming calls he saw on the phone screen.

Tony stretched his neck, feeling it crack and touched his shoulder.

* * *

The cold shower was soothing and Tony's mind wandered.

What's next?

He shook his head figuring the Romanos were wide open and would call the Saltinottis right away. It would be an all-out war and he needed every man including his nephew Luca's help to crush their rivals off, once and for all.

He messed up taking the Saltinotti girl to his bed. Vincent's lust had now got him to this point.

Luca Giuliani was in control of New York's suburbs and Tony knew it would take a great force to take on Jacopo & Johnny. More now than ever, Tony needed Sofia. He now knew the reason why she came to his bed.

Tony turned the shower's knob, turning off the water. He reached for his towel and began drying off.

When he exited the bathroom, he found Vanessa turning his bedroom upside down.

"What are you looking for?"

"My fucking phone, I can't fucking find it," Vanessa cried.

Tempers sure does run in her family, Tony thought as he observed Vanessa, in only panties, hopping around the room and bending over, her tits jerking and her perfectly shaped ass on full display.

Ignoring the panicking, Tony opened his wardrobe and began dressing. He rolled up his sleeves of his black shirt to his elbows and glanced in the direction of Vanessa, who was still ghastly turning every object in the room, causing a serious chaos.

"Vanessa."

She stopped and slowly met Tony's gaze.

"Si."

"You need to go home."

"Fuck Tony! You're throwing me out?"

"No, I'm not but you need to go. I have some business to attend to."

Vanessa finally found her phone seeing that Vincent had called her over a hundred times.

Vanessa then nodded, not knowing whether another option available, but she would obey.

"Okay, Tony! When can I see you again?"

"Soon, my love. Now hurry!"

26

SOFIA DID WHAT? PART 2

Upstate New York

Sofia Giuliani was tough, smart and knew what it took to lead her grandsons to consolidate the mob's power. It would take more than a gunfight to crack the stone front, and there it was. Kidnapping Jacopo's daughter wasn't the most honorable move, she had to admit, it was brilliant. In the business the families were involved, this would go a very long way. Very effective, like holding a blade to a man's throat and waiting for him to move so that its sharpness can pierce through the flesh.

I'm too old for this shit. Too old for these games these youngsters are all playing. I don't have a heart in it anymore.

Once upon a time, I cared about building an empire so no one could fuck with us, this was what I would have died for.

Sofia didn't give a fuck about any of her rivals past and present. It was about survival. She outlasted three generations of organized crime. She knew how to make it and not once did she get arrested.

She remembered Vanessa Saltinotti when she was a five-year-old, holding her father's hand while they exited church on a cloudy Sunday morning. Sofia could have ended Jacopo then but for the sake of faith, stopped short of her plans.

If there was a weapon that killed Sofia off in this game, it would've been her own. *The irony.*

The old woman shook her head, the corner of her lips tugging slightly, amused at the turn of events. She looked up and ahead across the many trees and fields in her late husband's mansion. *Tony and Luca really did well for themselves,* she thought, smoking a Marlboro.

The smoke escaped into the cool evening air that the summer presented. She enjoyed the settled temperature. Nothing like Manhattan, her neighborhood was cooler and quieter.

Finishing her cigarette, she walked past Luca's bedroom (he was out in New York with Tony) and down the hallway to the living room. She sat there for a few minutes and poured herself a glass of wine.

Sofia eyelids became heavier and she felt the urge of

sleep take over, her sharpness blurring. Then, she heard the sounds of footsteps, quickly reaching under the sofa for her Glock and in one motion, stood and aimed in the direction of the noise.

"Jesus Sofia, what the fuck are you doing!"

Sofia sighed at Nadia whom Tony had sent to cook for her this weekend while he and Luca took care of business. "What the fuck do you think you are doing, sneaking up on me?" Sofia scrunched at the chef and then plummeted back on the sofa.

Nadia couldn't help herself from staring at this beautiful old woman, eyeing her olive complexion.

"I just came to check up on you, Donna," Nadia said, taking a seat next to Sofia.

Sofia looked at Nadia, analyzing the chef. She then leaned to the corner of the sofa, resting her elbow on the arm and crossed her legs. "You know Nadia, I was wondering why a beautiful woman like you gave her life away to become the chef of Tony - I mean, surely you were renowned and considering your age, you still have a few more years left in the tank."

Nadia, whose hair was a mess and tussled across her face, sat staring at the floor while listening.

"What I think happened," Sofia continued without waiting for Nadia's response. "Was that you were in a predicament, not a normal one, more like an addiction, is that so?" Sofia shuffled closer. "But I think it might have been something more scandalous." She reached for Nadia's chin seeing her tears stream.

Sofia smiled at the poor middle-aged woman and stroked both her cheeks.

Nadia leaned into Sofia, it was comforting. It had been a very long time since the last time that someone offered such a gentle touch. She did not want it to end. She thought about Sofia's gentleness, needing for her to drop her hands slightly and cup her breasts—to squeeze them tightly and bring them further down past her stomach and pelvic mound.

"What was it that you needed Tony's help with?" Sofia said calmly, enjoying the fact that Nadia was clearly comforted. "Was it the fact that you messed with the wrong people and owed money?"

Nadia didn't give a hint away. "Donna—I…"

"Or was it the fact that you like sex too much?"

Nadia's eyes rolled away from her and Sofia decided to probe this a little more. "You were a freak perhaps?"

Before the sentence was completed, Sofia grabbed the hem of the cook's lengthy night gown and pulled it over her shoulder, exposing her cleavage and collar bone.

"Oh, Donna!"

"You wanted to be dominated. You enjoy being used and fucked, without anyone caring for you." Sofia ripped her shirt, causing a big tear right down the middle, Nadia's tits bounced in the open.

Sofia grabbed her nipple and pulled Nadia closer, their faces inches away and she enjoyed the face Nadia was putting on; closed eyes, mouth slightly open and her mind focusing on the pain. "You loved being the vessel people could use for their own pleasure, and then be tossed."

Sofia pushed Nadia down on her back and got in between her legs and kissed her. The kiss was passionate and fierce. Her hands started fondling with Nadia's panties ultimately removing them.

"I heard the sounds you made that night when I was over Tony's."

"Oh, Donna, yes!" Nadia panted as Sofia's lips went downward.

She moaned and couldn't help herself from biting down on her lips. "Please, Donna" she begged.

Sofia lowered herself until her tongue began licking Nadia's cunt, playing with her puffy lips and entering it and tasting her. She then fingered her perfectly and aggressively, feeling Nadia squirm under her control.

"How much do you want it?" Sofia asked.

The question registered with Nadia, but she had no authority or power to form an answer. Her lips were shaking from the incredible sensations her cunt was subjected to. Every lick was calculated, like Sofia knew where her weak points were precisely and the old woman was abusing them. Her legs began shivering and she squeezed inwards nearly crushing Sofia's head. Nadia moans grew louder and louder even causing the guards outside to chuckle.

"I asked you a question," Sofia said impatiently. "How much do you want it?"

"So much."

"What would you do for it?" Sofia asked.

Nadia gasped. "Anything you want, Donna."

"You are mine. You do want I tell you!" Sofia Giuliani said. "You hear me?"

"Si, Donna. Oh! Oh! Oh!"

Sofia smiled, lightly slapping Nadia's cunt. Seconds later, Nadia shrieked and came. What Sofia didn't expect was Nadia's cum to squirt on her face. It was a powerful blast as well.

Sofia wiped her face with Nadia's ripped nightgown, looking at her as Nadia was trying to catch her breath. She was an absolute mess.

"You're in for a night of trouble, Nadia. Now go to my room. We have a lot to talk about."

THE BOSSES MAKE A DEAL?

Manhattan, New York

A meeting was set between Don Johnny Romano and his son, Vincent in an empty warehouse in downtown Manhattan. Luca Giuliani and Tony arranged a plan devised by Sofia to get both at once.

The meeting place by New York Harbor was darkly lit and not decorated. Its walls were bare and painted in a boring beige, a few deep cracks giving them an artistic depth. A nasty smell lingered, a combination of urine and feces.

It was disrespectful to Tony, Luca, Don Johnny Romano & son to met in such a disgusting place but they didn't care. Business is business!

Tony pulled one of four old chairs out, and made himself at home.

After forty minutes and three cigarettes smoked, the door was opened and the same bulky guard who had opened the door for Tony and Luca, held it open for Vincent and his father, Johnny.

Not bothering to stand up and shake either man's hand, Tony and Luca seated studying every detail of the two. Johnny Romano had on an expensive suit and leather shoes, everything about him was sharp.

While his son, Vincent wore jeans, a hoodie and sneakers. He resembled a fat boxer.

"Vincent and Don Johnny," Tony said between exhaling the last of his cigarette. "What a pleasure to see you!"

"I wish I could say the same," Vincent said seeing the angry look his father gave him.

The four were now sat and silence encompassed the round table, their eyes flickered between one another. Tony stubbed his cigarette out. "Look, we're far off better as allies than we are as enemies."

"Get the fuck outta here. You fucked with wrong people, Tony. I will turn you into fucking shit until nobody can recognize you anymore. You don't get to treat my wife like a prostitute, threaten to release your porn video of her and then come here offering peace, you fucking cocksucker," Vincent said.

Tony looked at Luca and then at Johnny, wondering what the fuck did he just say.

"Vincent—Come on, buddy. We're here to make peace not war, right?" Luca said.

"Fuck you, Puta?"

"Hey—hey watch your mouth or else," Luca replied.

Vincent Romano was known for his short temper.

"If it is okay with you, Don Johnny, I would like to speak with you in private. Luca and Vincent can go talk like men outside."

"Ok, Tony." Johnny Romano turned to his son. "Leave us, son."

Vincent stood up, his chair dropping, and slammed his fists on the table. "You motherfucker, I'm not going anywhere, and you better give me my wife or else—"

"VINCENT," Don Johnny shouted.

Vincent looked at his father, his cheeks red and fists clenched. He shook his head and walked out with Luca.

* * *

"You've got what you wanted Tony," Don Johnny began. He spoke softly, choosing each word he spoke carefully. "You made your point." He cut a cigar and waved it beneath his nose, taking in its aroma. He then bit down on its end and held it to the fire of his chrome lighter. A few seconds and several puffs later, the cigar's thick smoke circulated the room.

"That was the wrong move, Johnny. Now, Jacopo wants war."

"I did not approve such stupidity, but unfortunately for all of us, my son seems to think it is acceptable to do whatever he likes without knowing consequences that can comeback and bite him in his arrogant ass."

"I agree," Tony's index reached his temple. "But you should have handled this better. You're still the Don."

"And I will continue to be—for the remaining of my time on Earth." Don Johnny let out a cloud of smoke. "Let Vanessa do what she wants. My son will be no more trouble."

Tony laughed. "You think that will solve the problem, huh?" He stood up glaring down at Johnny. "You're underestimating what your son has done. She's already home with her father. He's going to kill all of us." Tony reached for his Berretta, exposing its black metal. He then aimed and smiled.

"What the fuck is this, Tony? We said no guns."

"Let's just say that I know people in high places."

"You wouldn't, you piece of shit?"

"One has to pay for his sins. You have many!"

"Fuck you! I'm a made-man."

"That you were." Tony laughed, firing shot after shot at Don Johnny's head.

Tony reached for the Johnny's cigar, which had rolled across the floor, and placed it between his lips.

Footsteps were heard approaching the door.

Luca Giuliani came back with Vincent, his gun was drawn poked in his back.

"Care to join?" Tony smiled. "And before you lose your temper, let's not pretend you loved your father. You have wanted this for so long, and I am giving it to you on a silver platter."

Vincent's eyes crossed between him, Luca and the dead body of the great Don Johnny Romano. "You, motherfucker!"

"Let's talk business, shall we?" Tony passed the cigar over to Vincent and watched him hesitate, only to give in and smoke it anxiously, his eyes lowered to the floor.

"Luca, I think we might a deal that Vincent can't refuse, huh?"

"Si, nephew. Let's get back to business."

It didn't take long for hands to shake upon a new deal. Tony and Luca smiled at Vincent, who left with a blank expression. He made a deal with the devil while the body of his father was laying in the room.

2 8

THOSE COPPERS

Manhattan, New York

Tony and Luca were the last to come out of the warehouse. The moment they did, there were police cars everywhere. Tony, Luca, and their bodyguards raised their hands above their heads and turned around.

The ride to the police station was quick. The inside of the police car reeked of sweat, musk and piss. The car's police radio kept going off while Tony & Luca looked out the window. Their cuffs were on too tight.

"You two think just because you're wiseguys, you can get away with murder, huh?"

Tony and Luca rolled their eyes, peeping through

the metal brackets, to the passenger's side. The officer was fat, bald with a thick beard. His partner was the total opposite of him; a gym-rat and clean-shaven.

"We'll show you tow what the fuck's New York really about. You killed Johnny Romano? Bad mother-fucking move." The fat copper took out a bag of coke.

"Add that to the charges, boss," the driver said.

"Yeah, we might do just that. Everybody will want your heads. Better for you two to die inside the joint."

Tony and Luca didn't pay the coppers any mind.

They reached the police station and the fat cop and his partner dragged Tony and Luca out by their collars, pushing them forward. Then, the two were pushed down on the metal seats and handcuffed to poles underneath.

* * *

Hours went by and the officers in the station made them wait longer on purpose.

A black man was brought in and cuffed to a pole next to them.

"What you in here for man?"

"Shot somebody," Tony said.

"God damn, you two don't look like killers. You look like you belong in school."

Luca cocked an eyebrow at Tony. "So, what you in here for, brother?"

The man busted out in laughter. "Shit dawg, you see that lady over there." He nodded to a woman sitting across the room, wearing a mini-skirt, exposing her thighs. Her make-up was smudged and her hair was messy. She smiled at the man showing her stained teeth.

"She's your lady?" Tony said grimacing.

"Kind of man, but not like that, you think that low of me?"

Tony glanced at the man's clothing. "Should I?"

"Shit, at least you're honest, man. But nah, she's not my lady. That girl comes to my hotel room and hand me my money, you feel me?"

"You're her pimp," Luca said.

The man giggled."You quick man."

"How'd you get busted?" Tony said.

"She was on her knees, sucking some dick—man when the boys in blue pulled up."

"So how did you get arrested?"

"I was fucking that bitch from behind."

Tony palmed his forehead and began laughing. "You're right, this shit is hilarious."

All of them were laughing.

"Hey, you bozos over there. Knock it off!"

"Fuck you man," the black man yelled.

* * *

Another hour went by and Tony was called first. He was finally getting processed. His fingerprints were taken, mug shots and then the cops hauled him over to a payphone.

"One call is all you got, so better make it good."

Tony stretched his neck and shoulders. He knew who he would call punched the number in. The line rang until someone picked.

"Who is this?"

"Tony Lombardi."

There was a quick pause. "You know better to call me directly."

"I do, but got to call in that favor you owe me."

"You know what the price is."

"You're good. The shit I got on you will be destroyed but it's still some stuff in the pipes."

"I'll take my chances, what do you need?"

"A pardon."

The caller paused again. "I don't think I heard you correctly."

"I got booked for murder."

"You're not one to get arrested for icing somebody." The caller paused again. "Who'd you whack?"

"Johnny Romano."

"You've gotta be fucking kidding me."

"I wanna be out of here in the next 45 minutes, if I'm not I'll release the video of you fucking your dog and then your daughter. You can kiss your new political career goodbye. I won't stop there, you know me. I'll leave you fucking high and dry without a single penny. Now do it."

"Alright, alright, Jesus Christ." Was all the caller said. The line went dead.

Tony put down the receiver and was brought back to the same seat he previously occupied. Luca leaned over and asked, "Is it taken care of?"

"Yeah, we'll be outta here in an hour."

The black man and his woman were long gone, probably let go. Tony and Luca rested their head against the back of the seats and closed their eyes.

* * *

Forty-five minutes later, Tony first saw the same big copper whom arrested him and Luca, now in street clothes, his face was red. Tony and Luca knew what was coming.

The cop, in silence, uncuffed Tony and Luca, pocketed their handcuffs. "Have a good evening, Misters Lombardi and Giuliani. Your case has been removed, including your iris scans and fingerprints. You're free to go.

The men simply nodded.

"How did you get the DA to drop all charges?" The copper asked.

"I guess by being friends with the President," Tony said as he and Luca walked out of the police station.

HOME SWEET HOME

Upstate New York

There were several knocks on the door and it interrupted Sofia's sleep. She yawned and stretched, glancing over her shoulder seeing Nadia naked. Her fingers traced against the skin of her Tony's live-in chef. *He'd be pissed off about the encounter?*

Sofia then stretched and whimpered slightly to the door putting on her robe.

She couldn't believe her own eyes.

"Hi, Sofia." Vanessa awkwardly, laughing at the messy sight that Sofia was.

"What are you doing here, Saltinotti?"

"Well, I wanted to thank you for saving my life. My

husband—I mean ex-husband, Vincent divorced me, so I'm moving in."

"What the—?"

"By the way, I picked up Tony and Luca from the police station."

"Move aside. Where are they?"

Vanessa smiled stepping aside. Sofia squinted realizing her boys were sitting in the Mercedes - parked awkwardly on the round driveway. The back door opened and Luca got out first.

"Miss me much, Nonna?" Luca said.

"What are you doing with Vanessa? We're at war!"

"Nonna, we took care of everything. Don't worry. Go back to sleep."

Sofia rolled her eyes as the two men came inside with Vanessa.

3 0

THE END OF A DON

New York City, USA

Six months later

Luca Giuliani's right hand bled; deep cuts over its knuckles as blood dripped onto the floor. He sighed punching the man over and over again, feeling his teeth crack, and lip split. When Luca was tired, he told his men he was going to take a break.

That man was Jacopo Saltinotti, the retired mob boss.

"Let him down," Luca said.

One of his men moved to the chain and let it loose, letting the old mob boss, who had spent the last twenty-four hours in the air chained to opposite walls and neck

151

to the ceiling, without water or any food, getting punched by many different men. Jacopo was barely hanging on for dear life.

Luca gulped down a glass of wine and wiped his mouth with his forearm. "Take care of him will you, he's a thing of the past." He put on his jacket, struggling to button it up.

A gunshot followed and Luca prayed silently.

He was sweating bullets, breathing heavily as he came up from the basement. The air outside was a relief. The young Giuliani stood in the sunshine, with his eyes closed, not knowing how long he would stand there for. The war was over and he just tied up the loosest end.

When he opened his eyes, they locked on with his uncle Tony's.

"When did you get here?"

"Paul brought me over. I didn't want to miss the funeral."

"The job's done. Sorry, Zio."

"You really suck!"

"I know but I got something else for us to do. Let me get dressed. We're going to get fucking laid."

Minutes later, Paul, Luca, and Tony took off.

* * *

"Where would you like to go today, boss?" Luca's driver said.

"Take us to the fucking whores in Chinatown," Luca yelled.

"Si, Boss."

Tony had to admit that he was thinking the same thing.

"Hey Zio, They got Thai, Chinese, Japanese, Vietnamese and girls from the Philippines."

Luca closed his eyes, picturing the girls.

"Let's get fucked then. Look at my fucking hand, Zio."

"Damn, you really are beating that old man to his grave," Tony snickered.

"The same as last time boss?" the driver interrupted.

"Si," Tony said.

"How's Vanessa? You know she's carrying the next Don of New York?"

"Yeah, Zio. That Saltinotti gets on my fucking nerves asking for this and that. The girl is a fucking brat."

"I know. I saw her little sister, Lucia downtown last week. Man, she's growing some tits."

"You crazy, Zio. I didn't tell you but I fucked their mother."

"Get the fuck outta here!"

"Maria needed a favor. Let's just say I took care of her."

Luca's phone rang. "Give me a second. I need to take this."

THE CHINATOWN SETUP - PART 2

Chinatown, New York

One of Luca's bodyguards looked at the building's camera before calling upstairs. "Got two, boss."

"Perfect, send them up. Take a break, we'll be okay," Luca said.

"Ok, Boss."

Minutes later, the girls came in. They were beautiful almost looking like twin sisters with their matching slutty outfits. Both were wearing red heels that were six inches maybe.

"My God!" Luca whispered to Tony. The women approached kissing them both on the cheek.

"Zio, we're going to have fun with these hoes," Luca said going to the kitchen and bringing back two bottles of wine. Meanwhile, Tony stayed with the women.

Luca returned and they ogled the two Chinese girls, fully dressed but standing awkwardly.

"What are you waiting for? Take your fucking clothes off!" Tony yelled.

The girls began removing their heels as Luca and Tony watched them. The duo smiled as the two girls then went to take off their tops. Their fake tits had jiggled around and Tony and Luca were already turned on.

The girls teased them, shaking their asses, giggling.

"Yeah, mama! Give us more," Luca said.

Luca and Tony stroked their cocks.

"We said take it all off, bitches. We want to fuck—"

The girls slowly began pulling down their skirt but something was strange; one pulled down hers all the way and the other did not.

"Oh shit, fucking ladyboys, Zio!" Tony said. "What the fuck?"

One of the girls quickly pulled out two guns with silencers from her back. She handed one to her companion.

"Mr. Zhang, our late father says, "Hello from his grave!"

"Who the fuck is Mr. Zhang?" Luca shouted.

The girls shot Luca and Tony in the head once and walked out calmly, closing the door.

157

The End